BROODING

YA HERO

Becoming a
MAIN CHARACTER
(Almost) as
AWESOME AS ME

BROODING YA HERO

Becoming a MAIN CHARACTER (Almost) as AWESOME AS ME

CARRIE DiRISIO ILLUSTRATED BY LINNEA GEAR

SKY PONY PRESS

Sky Pony Press
New York

Visit our website at www.skyponypress.com

www.creativelycarrie.com
www.thebroodingyahero.tumblr.com
linneart.tumblr.com

10 9 8 7 6 5 4 3 2 1

Library of Congress Cataloging-in-Publication Data available on file.

Jacket illustration by Linnea Gear
Jacket design by Sammy Yuen

Hardcover ISBN: 978-1-5107-2666-6
Ebook ISBN: 978-1-5107-2671-0

Printed in the United States of America

Interior design by Joshua L. Barnaby

*To everyone who's ever wanted to be the star of their own story.
Here's a spoiler: you already are.*

*And to my family, full of storytellers and comedians,
who taught me to laugh and love.*

What's in a name? That which we call a main character
By any other name would be as awesome.
(But they wouldn't be on the cover of the book.)

See? Doesn't that Shakespeare quote make
me look super-literary and very talented?

Baddy

CONTENTS

PROLOGUE

Alone in his room, Broody McHottiepants contemplated his future. He was the best of all fictional characters ever created—that he knew. His phone never stopped ringing (playing his theme song, from his latest hit movie adaptation, of course) with Authors begging him to star in their latest novels. An endlessly talented man, he'd been everything from a vampire to a quarterback. Into each novel, he brought his incredibly adjective-filled beauty; his gemstone-colored gaze; his strong, strong arms; and his potent blend of wish fulfillment and slightly toxic masculinity.

And each time, people swooned.

Everyone loved him. He'd recently opened a Twitter account, and there, loyal fans waited for him to speak his beautiful, vivid, wondrous wisdom. As the hero of so many stories, he was uniquely qualified to share the brilliant advice everyone adored:

Brooding YA Hero
@broodingYAhero

I'm a powerful immortal male but I only pursue teen girls for my love interests. If I was 43 instead of 430 years old, this would be creepy.

Brooding YA Hero
@broodingYAhero

Is a good relationship based on mutual trust and friendship?
No way.
The best relationships are built on mutual disdain and smirking.

Brooding YA Hero
@broodingYAhero

One of my greatest talents in life is my ability to tell you just enough about your past/magical powers/my love life to ensure a sequel.

Brooding YA Hero
@broodingYAhero

It's a well-known fact that every successful fictional monarchy accidentally misplaces a princess every century or so.

Sure, he'd had movie and TV deals, too. Even comic books. He'd overthrown evil dystopian governments, won the state championship in sportsball, and always, *always* found true love.

And yet, something wasn't right. Not today. It wasn't a usual day in New Story City, the place where all character archetypes, from the wisest, oldest mentors to the youngest, annoying-est siblings, waited for Authors to draft them into new stories.

Most mornings, Broody woke to a summons from an Author. Depending on the type of story, it might arrive by text message, or by carrier pigeon. Reality shifted easily in New Story City.

But it had been two weeks, and still no Author had contacted him.

Two whole weeks without saving the world, or sulking in the middle of a dramatic landscape, or trading sarcastic barbs with a villain. Sure, New

Story City offered some minor distractions—other characters to talk to, gyms where he could work on his flawless abs—but life was *so* boring when he wasn't starring in a book.

So Broody did what any frustrated fictional character might do when in need of some screen time and adoring fans.

He complained to everyone he knew.

Finally, after sending over thirteen mopey tweets, blasting whiny music, and sighing dramatically whenever anyone said hi, Broody's phone rang.

His phone was a rather amorphous object, as writers could never keep up with how quickly technology changed, but the important thing was that it worked.

"Yo," he said, and then cursed his unfortunate habit of relying on outdated slang. Publishing was a slow business, and sometimes a character's dialogue paid the price.

The voice on the other end of the line crackled, and Broody felt a very unlike-him shiver race down his spine. He was a hero. He didn't shiver. That stuff was for girls. But when the voice spoke, he was right to be afraid. For it was the most powerful, the most dangerous, of all beings.

It was an Author.

"Broody," the Author said. "We need to talk."

And Broody, who lived in fear of all direct communication, and most especially that specific phrase, felt the world swim around him.

The Author's words turned to a dull echo in Broody's brain, reverberating around the rather empty space in there.

But he comprehended enough.

Broody was being . . . dumped.

"You see, it's just . . ." The Author paused. "There are so many other stories to tell, Broody. You don't need to star in all of them."

"But I'm the best."

"You are . . . You are something, Broody."

"Did I do something wrong?" Well. That was a given. He usually did at least fifteen things wrong per book, but only in a swoony, romantic way, where all could be fixed when he took off his shirt.

The Author took a deep breath. "It's not you, Broody. It's me."

"I knew it!" He beamed, triumphant. "See. It's all your fault. A different Author could have written such masterpieces with my magnificent manly self."

"You know what? I lied. It is you, not me, Broody."

The phone went silent.

Broody was too heartbroken to even come up with some amazing turn of phrase about how its silent emptiness mirrored that which lay deep in his soul.

Broody had done nothing, not even brooded or sulked, for hours. Time passed, and outside, in his city full of other characters, life happened. Heroes would be summoned to stories. Villains would plot. Love interests would swoon. Adorable street-rat orphans would pick pockets.

But Broody would do . . . nothing.

No more stories?

For how long?

What could he do?

Broody was very good at moping, and even better at brooding. But eventually, even for him, that grew boring.

What were his other talents? Smirking while defeating evil forces? Clenching his jaw dramatically while threatened by said evil forces? Ignoring love interests until page 201?

Well, yes. All of those things. He was very talented.

But certainly, he also had great skill with narrative, and an amazing degree of creativity. Adjectives and adverbs abounded in his interior monologue, and he mixed metaphors like a DJ.

With all that in mind . . . why, he didn't need an Author! He was Broody McHottiepants. He could write his own book.

Writing had always seemed . . . well . . . Book writing, like painting, dancing, and having empathy, was a hobby best left to his love interests.

But why not? Why shouldn't he record his memoirs so that everyone could bask in his brilliance? Wouldn't it show the Author how vital he was if he,

Broody McHottiepants, wrote and starred in his own book?

How hard could it be? Authors wrote books about *him* all the time.

So, Broody sat down and began to write.

A BRIEF HISTORY OF THE LIFE OF ME, BROODY McHOTTIEPANTS, MORE COMMONLY KNOWN AS BROODING YA HERO

Hello, dear reader, and thank you for gazing into my beautiful, crisp, linen-soft, sweetly scented pages. The swoon-producing effect they will have on you is far milder than the impact of one second spent entranced by my steely, azure-tinged emerald orbs but, alas, it will have to do.

In these pages, I will attempt to reveal to you all my secrets. From my favorite recipe to my least favorite plot device, I will tell you everything your desperate heart desires.

Provided your heart desires only me.

It does, right?

Look, I'm not going to spend the whole book wondering if I'm in a love triangle. I'm way too important for that. Please check the below box with your answer to this question:

Are you deeply in love with me?

☐ Yes
☐ Mostly yes
☐ Always and forever
☐ At least until the sequel

Good. That was the right answer. I permit you to keep reading.

I'd like to tell you a bit about myself. Apparently, some "Authors" put an About Me at the end of the book. That's totally stupid. *Obviously*, everyone is only reading this book to learn all about me, including how many adjectives have been used to describe my eye color (12,887), just how strong my arms are (so, so strong), and my favorite food (the homemade cookies you'll make for me to prove how much you love me). (P.S. I may even give you my favorite cookie recipe in this book.)

So, ahem. More about me. I am the brooding hero found in all your favorite books, from that lush, dramatic fantasy trilogy you adored, to the contemporary, swoony romance that made you giggle. I come from a long line of brooding heroes—Romeo's little brother (as poor, dear, dead Great-Great-Uncle Romy had some . . . uh, bad luck with plot twists) on my mother's side, and Fitzwilliam Darcy on my father's. We still sometimes summer at Pemberley, when I remember to be very British. (Not English, mind you. My Author isn't aware there's a difference.)

Perhaps this is already confusing to you. How could I be both your British boyfriend and your all-American football star? Well, you see, as a brooding hero character archetype, I can recall every story I've ever been in. Whenever an Author creates a character that fits my personality, the Author is actually directly summoning me, and I awaken inside the story. This same phenomenon occurs with other characters, like my evil ex-girlfriend, Blondie DeMeani, but let's keep our focus on the most important topic.

Me.

While starring in so many stories and inhabiting so many fictional worlds, I've learned a great deal. I've ruled kingdoms and toppled dystopian regimes, won sportsball championships and starred in musicals. Every single time, my main character attributes—my beautiful, intense gaze; my manly clenched jawline; and my rather oddly attractive arrogance—has won over the hearts of readers everywhere. And winning readers' hearts is the number one best thing to do if you want a sequel.

So, why should you keep reading this book? Haven't you ever wanted to know what it feels like to be a character inside your favorite stories? Or wanted to learn how to survive and thrive in sequels? Or how to identify an antagonist from a hundred yards away? At the very least, don't you want to spend more time with me when you're awake and not just when I'm romantically/creepily/obsessively watching you slumber from outside your window?

As I've already said but will say again, I've been in quite a few stories, and I know everything about them. By reading this fantastic, brilliant book about me and my life, why, I'm sure you'll improve your own, at least a smidgen.

In fact, I've had the most genius idea. Why don't I just interview myself!

Broody: Well, Mr. McHottiepants, your résumé is certainly impressive. Have you really been in *all* of these stories?

Me: Absolutely. In fact, I've been in all their film adaptations, plus plenty of TV shows and movies that didn't begin as books. One might even venture to say I've existed as far back as the earliest known stories, although I refuse to talk about that since I made some unfortunate choices about wardrobe and girlfriends . . .

Broody (a.k.a. Me):   **What's your favorite role?**

Also Me: Being the hero, of course. But, no. I shall never name my favorite book. I can't have armies of love interests from my billions of starring roles band together to jealously hunt me down. Thank goodness they're all "not like other girls" and, thus, will always refuse to work with other women.

Me: Let's go back to the more basic questions, shall we?

Also Me: Brilliant idea, Broody.

Me: Why, thank you. I've been known to have a few.

Also Me: **What's your name?**

Me: Broody McHottiepants. Occasionally, I am Prince Broody, Rather-too-young-to-be-a-military-leader Broody, or Master Mage and Sassmaster Broody.

Oh, and I was either named after my father (who I dislike greatly) or was given a very fitting epitaph that my Author found in a baby name dictionary.

Or a noun. Sometimes I'm named after a manly, sexy noun. Jet. Blaze. Hunter. Smoke. Trout.

Also Me: **When were you born?**

Me: Before you, duh. I'm always older. And taller.

Also Me: **Favorite color?**

Me: The black darkness of my heart. Or the fiery red of my passion.

Also Me: **Where do you live?**

Me: Anywhere—from the finest palace to the roughest dystopian cave. No matter where I find myself, however, I have access to an excellent barber and top-notch dental care. This tousled mane and blazing smile don't maintain themselves, you know.

Also Me: **Hobbies?**

Me: Fighting. Sulking. Causing drama by lying to people I care about. I'm also ridiculously good at anything I attempt, including fencing, poker, playing all musical instruments, insulting girls in a way they will find complimentary, sportsball, fixing cars, fixing a girl's emotional distress (oftentimes caused by me—also a great hobby), overthrowing governments, and throwing masquerade balls.

Oh, and smirking. Can't forget the smirking.

One thing I don't do? Read. That's for main female characters only.

Also Me: **Favorite subject in school?**

Me: Really? You're asking me that? I thought you knew me, self. I thought we had a connection. I'm not even going to honor that with a response.

Also Me: **What are you afraid of?**

Me: Absolutely nothing.

Okay . . . Maybe once in a while I have a nightmare that I'll lose a love triangle, or worse, that my book will never get a sequel, but I'm pretty darn confident those are just nightmares, and not the sort of dream that foretells exactly what will happen in my fictional future.

Also Me: **Zodiac sign?**

Me: After hours and hours of careful consideration (which definitely had nothing to do with deadline-based procrastination, thank you very much), my Author has decided I am a Scorpio. This is because Scorpios are the perfect fit for any broody hero: passionate, deadly, and totally overused in fiction.

However, my Author is still researching my Chinese zodiac sign, my Myers-Briggs personality type, my ideal tarot card, my blood type, and my Hogwarts house. These are all 100 percent vital to the development of any main character. So if you, too, aspire to achieve main character status, be sure to complete as many online quizzes as possible while you wait for your destiny to make itself apparent.

Also Me: **What do you want to be when you grow up?**

Me: The husband of a main character.

Also, a very rich rock star/king/vampire lord/artist/athlete. I'm pretty flexible. As long as I end the book as the most important guy in the whole world, I'll settle for any career, really. But you know who I hope I never become? My father. He's the worst. He thinks everything is always about him and has no sympathy for anyone else, especially not me. Granted, he's also ridiculously wealthy and very handsome, but he's a jerk. So, I just want to be way better than him.

Also Me: **Favorite movie?**

Me: Something from the '80s. Probably with John Cusack in it.

There's a slight chance I might like a nerdy movie, like *Star Wars* or *Star Trek* or *Stargate* or *Stardust* or . . . But, really, that kind of thing is more for my ultimate rival, Nice Guy Next Door.

Also Me: **Favorite music?**

Me: Something from the '80s.

I'm really hip. All the coolest modern main characters love stuff from the '80s. That has absolutely nothing to do with my Author's age. It's just, you know, because I'm really rad, and down with it, and totally phat.

My obviously-up-to-date slang is also the bee's knees, smoothalicious, totally radical. You dig?

Also Me: **Least favorite person?**

Me: My father. My rival. My best friend (if he hits on my love interest). My teachers, who actually expect things of me, which is really rude of them. That one guy who spoke to my love interest once.

Actually, no. I know my least favorite person. . . . It's my love interest's annoying best friend, who says totally untrue things like "I think Broody's bad for you," or "You should go to class more often," or "I don't think it's healthy to make your life revolve around a guy you just met."

I mean, seriously. Who does that girl think she is? A main character? Absolutely not.

Also Me: **What do you look for in a girlfriend?**

Me: I have very deep feelings on this, so I've dedicated a whole section of the book to this topic. Please turn to page 163.

But, in short, I'm looking for a clumsy girl who is ridiculously good at describing my eye color, and is so clueless that she can make a simple plot drag out for three books (and four movies).

Also Me: **Ideal first date?**

Me: Saving prom/battle of the bands/the world. Alternatively, doing something incredibly romantic for my love interest, and then refusing to speak to her for the next fifty-three pages.

Or, you know, just staring into her eyes until our heartbeats synchronize. For details about romance, see book section How Can You Create Love?" on page 170.

Also Me: **You look great! I mean, we look great, right? We're just the best-looking guy to ever have existed in a high school setting (potentially due to the fact that we're played by a twenty-something actor). How did you get into such awesome shape?**

Me: First of all, thanks, but duh. Of course I look great. I'm the hottest guy in school/the kingdom/Hollywood for a reason.

My workout routine includes eyebrow lifts (for maximum quirking potential), leaping over plot holes, high-jumping to conclusions, bench-pressing my emotions to make them easier to suppress, and climbing up cliffs I've been left hanging on.

Also Me: **Broody, what's your deepest secret?**

Me: I . . . I just . . . I can't tell you yet.

Also Me: **Maybe later?**

Me: I just don't know if I can trust anyone. Perhaps, if people really want to know, they should first let out the breaths they didn't know they were holding and begin reading this magical book I'm writing. Then they'll learn just how dangerous I am. And, if they're still brave enough to hold my gemstone gaze for an excessively long time, I'll think about telling them the truth.

So, although this book is called *Brooding YA Hero: Becoming a Main Character (Almost) as Awesome as Me*, I think it's important to note that there is one type of main character that is far, far more important, more vital, more beautiful than any other.

That is, a Brooding Hero.

Now that you've gotten to know me, you're probably pretty jealous. It's okay. It happens to all of us. You wouldn't believe how many Nice Guys Next Door have shouted at me, frustrated by my absolute perfection. Characters I've only met once challenge me to duels to prove they are no less attractive than I am. Even evil overlords dedicate a massive amount of time to sulking over my amazing ability to deliver quippy one-liners while fighting their minions. But, because you're reading my incredible novel, I am going to magnanimously reveal some tips on how you can be broodier (although let's be honest: you'll never be on my level, as I am the true Broody, the Chosen Broodster, the best ever).

Before I begin, I warn you that being a Broody will change your life, so this is not a decision to be made lightly. Clumsy main characters will trip and fall into your arms. Random exes will reappear in your life and detail their plans to win you back.

Plot-specific prophecies will echo in your ears, reminding you of the destiny you've been trying to avoid your whole life. Puppies, plot devices, and small children will follow you around. And your clothing budget will skyrocket, because every time you pose dramatically for a book cover, all your buttons will fly off.

Maybe that's just me. Book covers always confuse me anyway, especially when I look completely different from how the Author describes me on the page.

But if you're absolutely sure that you're ready to grow your broodiness, even after all of my extremely generous cautions, then keep reading. (But don't say I didn't warn you.)

1. **Intensify your expressions.**
   No one wants a Broody who just "frowns" or "shrugs." Make sure to add adverbs to everything you do. Bonus points if your expressions involve your eyebrows. Which would you rather do: "sneeze" or "wrinkle your handsome Romanesque nose, your chestnut eyebrows leaping in masculine surprise as you dramatically detect the offending scent of pepper invading your beautiful nostrils"?

2. **Revel in descriptive actions.**
   Don't "wash the dishes" like a supporting character. Instead, be sure to "slowly, with

callused, strong hands, submerge each dish, as white and smooth as bone, into the glistening, lavender-scented water, while your eyebrow lifts quizzically at the concept of housework."

3. **Hug people, but only if they're short and your heartbeats synchronize easily.**
Be sure the person notices your strong arms. They *must* be described as strong, or how will this tiny main character you're embracing feel safe? I recommend doing at least three push-ups per day to ensure strong triceps. You simply don't have time for a longer gym workout; you'll be too busy brooding, partying, and suppressing your feelings.

4. **Tousle your hair.**
I'm not exactly sure what this means, but I'm certain that tousled hair is much broodier than untousled. No matter how long you're on the run from evil forces, as a Broody, your hair will never grow too long to simply shake out of your face (or you have a magic teleporting barber, who the reader never sees), which is very convenient. Don't be worried if your hair "shades your eyes." It will never actually obscure your vision, though it will do wonders to obscure your true motives from your love interest.

5. **Find a manly hobby that will come in handy exactly once in the plot.**
Examples include: lock-picking, automotive repair, and baking the perfect pie crust.

6. **Take up multiple bad habits that will in no way hamper you in the course of the plot, though they would in real life.**
Even if you smoke, you'll never be short of breath when you're running for your life. Likewise, hangovers only exist for female characters. As a man, you're much too manly to face adverse effects from dangerous, possibly illegal activities.

    Heck, you're even the only teenager who has absolutely zero problem driving any automobile ever. You were flawlessly parallel parking the day *before* you got your license.

    Wait. Who am I kidding? Fictional characters don't take driving tests. We're given personality appropriate cars.

7. **Find exactly one humorous friend.**
Two would just be excessive. Three would make it look like you're in a comedy troupe. There is nothing swoony about a comedy team.

8. **Prepare a large reserve of witty comebacks.**
You may need to steal these from aforementioned funny friend. Use your clever quips

often, especially in situations where you'd
never have time to say something amusing
and sarcastic in real life. For example, if
you're in the middle of an epic sword fight,
both you and your enemy should probably
be gasping for breath. But a true Broody
will effortlessly summon the breath necessary to issue a scathing insult about your
opponent's hair.

9. **Glare.**
At your teacher. At your reflection. At the
weather. There is nothing in the world that
can't be made broodier with a good, deep,
adverb-laced glare.

   Here, take a moment to practice. See that
smug, handsome guy on the cover? That's
me. Give me your best glare possible, and
see if it can make me blink.

   If I don't blink, you've got a lot more
work to do.

10. **When in doubt, lean and smirk.**
The lean-and-smirk fits any situation. The
villain threatens you? Slowly cross your
arms, lean back, and smirk. You don't have
your homework? Lean against a desk and
smirk. Your love interest confesses she
wants to be with you forever? Yup. Lean and
smirk. Works every time.

There you have it. A list of handy tips to increase your brooding potential. But though you may be able to apply the above practices to become *more* broody, only *I* can be *the* Broody. Please don't become overconfident and attempt to make love interests swoon with only a smirk. Even for me, there are various levels of brooding. As a main character, I answer to all summons from Authors, even when they aren't quite sure they need someone of my incredible level of broodosity.

The first level is the **Hot Guy with Brooding Moments**. This level of Broody is required when the Author is trying very hard to be "discreet." That's a very silly word that means there won't be many extra adjectives or ridiculously dramatic moments in this story.

Anyway, this guy is one good-looking, cool guy. He's probably lacking a bit in the adjectives department, and may potentially even be able to communicate his emotions effectively. Poor guy. He'll never be the best Broody he can be if he actually has conversations with his love interest. But, as he is still someone with Brooding Moments, he'll manage a few things to make me proud. For example, he'll have at least one excellent sulking scene and a few places where he can display his manly rage. Maybe he'll even get a chance to let the flecks of gold in his eyes sparkle.

The next level is an **Intentional Broody**. In this instance the Author, aware of how wonderful

I am, wishes for me to imbue the story with my incredible talents. This is the first level of Broody at which an Author personally requests that I, Broody McHottiepants, appear. The Author is careful to depict me with lots of adjectives, give me plenty of romantic moments, and at least fifteen occasions in which I refuse to discuss my emotions.

Next up is the **Sequel Upgrade Broody**. This is when a "Hot Guy with Brooding Moments" or another male character . . . morphs into me in the sequel. Confused? The conversation usually goes like this:

Author: Broody, my book is just so boring.

Me: Well, have you considered adding more adjectives? Maybe a song lyric or two at the beginning to make it look all fancy?

Author: I've already done that.

Me: How about a dream sequence? Those spice things up.

Author: I already have six!

Me: Hmm . . .

Author: Save me, Broody! You're my only hope.

Me: I am a very, very busy character, you know. But I suppose . . .

(And here I pause for great dramatic effect.)

I can become that random hot guy in your first book. Make him more . . . well, me. Which will, therefore, make the book less boring.

Author: THANK YOU, BROODY.

And so, I become the guy who previously was both boring and rational, and make him into someone far more dramatic, swoony, and all-around interesting.

Usually, the fans don't even notice.

But that is not the pinnacle of my abilities. Once in a great while, an Author seeks to . . . create the most **Broody of all Broodys**. To summon all of my blazing, brilliant power into one story. This Author risks life, limb, and readability in order to give me the most dramatic scenes, the most incredibly descriptive phrases, and all the dialogue tags I can dream of. It is truly, truly a wonderful role to play.

Note: I did not include the **Character People Wish Was a Broody**. This awkward situation happens occasionally, when an Author creates a character who they are absolutely sure is not a Broody. Oftentimes, he's a supporting villain or maybe he's barely even a supporting character. (That should be a big enough clue that I could never be him. I'm deeply allergic to playing a supporting character role.) But then, something unexpected happens, like a very, very handsome actor plays him in the movie version. Suddenly, all readers of the book expect this character to be . . . well . . . me. Ignoring that the character has done very little to be a Broody in the text, fans will give him all those brilliant talents I mentioned above. Sometimes, the Author gives in, allowing me to be this character in the sequel but, more often, the Author ignores the fans, and I feel caught in limbo between the desires of my demanding public and the Author's. It's not fun.

I mean, it's great to get all the awesome fan art and fanfic (more about that later) written about me-as-the-character-I-am-not, but I'd rather just be the star without ever sharing my spotlight.

Now, you may have noticed that I have not referred to any Authors by name. That is a personal choice. All Authors are powerful, godlike beings, who are capable of doing horrible things to characters. They can even delete us! And very few Authors ever write only one book. Therefore, in an effort to protect myself, I have vowed to never mention Authors' names as I share with you all their secrets.

Also, should you happen to meet an Author, would you mind informing them how brilliant, talented, and wonderful I am?

Maybe even slip them my number?

Thanks, reader. You rock.

NARRATIVE INTERLUDE: EVIL APPEARS!

There. The book was done. With at least twenty-seven adjectives and more than thirty perfectly necessary adverbs, it was certain to be a best-seller. Broody smiled at his masterpiece, his work of art, his autobiography. It was perfect. He should frame it. Or publish it. Maybe both.

But the room suddenly went cold, washed in a foreboding doom that smelled faintly of strawberry lip gloss. The air carried with it the sweet sounds of last year's biggest pop hit. Broody gasped, grabbed his book, and leapt to his feet. Only one character could be identified by her makeup right from the start of the novel. Good female characters always waited until after the plot dictated a makeover to start dressing up.

Only one character could make Broody quake in his (manly, and metaphorical) boots.

Blondie DeMeani appeared. He'd been right to be afraid.

As always, she was dressed flawlessly, perfectly made up, her blonde hair in lovely ringlets. No matter the time period or setting, Blondie always shone like a radioactive star that would probably kill you if you got too close. Broody would know. Blondie was . . . his evil ex-girlfriend.

Unlike a heroine, Blondie knew she was beautiful and flaunted it. Not one for non descript adjectives, or mousey hair, she held her head high, like she deserved to be noticed. That, in part, was one of the many reasons why she was pure evil. Self-confidence in a female character was just horrifying. And if that weren't evil enough, Blondie had also been known to have her own motivations, which sometimes included ignoring Broody's own goals. And she'd even kissed multiple guys other than Broody! Sometimes, she became stronger and more powerful after she'd gotten dumped. Totally ridiculous. Everyone knows that a woman with a broken heart should melt into a soft, mushy puddle of complete passivity in order to let plot happen.

Truly, Blondie was an archvillain. All of New Story City feared her sarcasm, her wrath, and her shopping sprees.

"What are you doing?" she asked Broody.

"I—I am . . ." He set his chin. "I am writing a book about how to become the most broody you can be."

He folded his arms. "And about being a hero. Which you would know nothing about."

But when her eyebrow arched, Broody stepped back. He wasn't scared. It would be ridiculous to be scared of a girl. He just moved backward because it was a cool thing to do, not because he was retreating.

"Sure," Blondie purred. She was always purring. He sometimes wondered if she was a werekitten. "Of course you can write a book about yourself. That's your favorite topic."

"It *is* not!" he thundered, his eyes flashing. Broody was 5 percent rain cloud, on his father's side. "I . . . have lots of other favorite topics."

Her eyebrow quirked even higher. Broody cursed the fact she had gotten better marks than him in Eyebrow Expressions 101. Finally, she said, "Like what?"

"True love?"

"So you're supportive of your love interest and that other guy in the love triangle finding happiness? Or your love interest running off with some other character who isn't you?"

Broody clenched his fists. No. That wasn't okay at all. How could he appear in the sequel if he was written out of the love triangle? He needed to be the hero of *all* relationships. It wasn't about his ego; it was about preserving the main character status quo.

"Maybe," Blondie said, "you should tell the reader how to become a main character."

"What?" Broody's eyebrows knitted together. Good. Finally, he'd remembered an expression from Eyebrow Class. Now, Blondie would remember he was a character not to be trifled with. Only the most badass characters got to have dynamic eyebrows. "Why would I do that?"

"Have you ever spoken to a supporting character?"

"Uh. Sure. Lots of times. You know, I ask them things like 'Hey, what's that cute new girl's name?' or 'Yo, dude, give me a compliment.'"

Blondie's eyebrow stayed lifted like a golden arch of judgment. "Wow. Those must be some fascinating conversations."

"What else am I supposed to ask a supporting character about?" They didn't have hopes or dreams or even the possibility of becoming a love interest.

"I don't know. Have you ever considered treating them like every other character?" Blondie drawled, studying her nails. They were, of course, painted the perfect shade for her—the bloodred of her enemies. Broody would know. He was usually her enemy.

"No, because they're supporting characters." Broody spoke the words slowly, confused why Blondie was finding this such a hard concept to grasp.

Oh.

Right.

Though she sometimes played the role of the antagonist, usually Blondie was just a supporting character. She never had an arc or plot points or any character growth. Once in a while, the narrative taught her a lesson or punished her for partying and being a badly behaved teen.

Of course, the story never did that to him. Mainly because he was a dude, and therefore infinitely better than any female character.

Blondie made a great show of checking her non-existent watch. "You done interior monologuing? Honestly, you main characters spend longer doing that than actually solving plot problems."

"Yeah, well, at least we get to actually have plot," he shot back. She flinched, pain widening her eyes. He must have struck a nerve he never knew she had. "I'm sorry. I . . . it's just . . . weird being visited by my evil ex-girlfriend."

Blondie paced around the room, examining the souvenirs and trophies from his billions of main character moments. "Broody, why am I so evil?"

"Well, you're really good-looking, and you know it." But after he responded, he realized he didn't know what she'd meant. Was Blondie's evil like his brooding? A very part of her being? Or did he just think she should be evil?

Ugh. He needed to get back in a book, and soon. He'd started an interior monologue like some wishy-washy main female character. Blondie was evil. Period.

A mirror flashed in front of him. Blondie spun it to show him his own reflection. "And you're not good-looking?"

"Uh, well." He rubbed his neck, and took a moment to shoot finger guns at the dashing guy in the mirror before replying. "You're also very rich."

"Yeah, so are you."

"I guess." Broody turned away from his reflection, though it was very difficult to stop staring into those beautiful lapis lazuli orbs, and went to his desk. "Blondie, you're an ambitious, beautiful, powerful woman. You're never going to be a protagonist."

She whirled on her heel. "Just go back to writing your stupid book, Broody."

The door slammed shut behind her.

THE INTERLUDE CONTINUES: GO TO SLEEP, PLOT COMING!

Blondie couldn't be right. There was no way. Broody had done what he'd set out to do. He'd written a book. Well, a very short book. But the very best book in all of New Story City.

He riffled through the pages again, considering the facts. He had yet to receive another call from an Author. He'd yet to awaken in another story.

And if he gave away even more secrets of becoming broody . . . there would never be a place for him in a story again.

So maybe it was necessary to shift focus. Only a little, and not because Blondie had suggested it. He'd simply do what Authors did and make a quick revision.

He flipped to the end of his notebook, tore out a page, scribbled something on it, and tucked it under his pillow. Then, he took a nap.

Every main character knows that falling asleep is the best way to speed up a boring part of a story.

When he woke up, he rustled under the pillow, for the paper. "Aha!" He held it aloft, triumphant. "A mysterious prophecy, delivered to me in the nick of time!"

All prophecies were incredibly convenient like that. The prophecy read:

Broody McHottiepants, hottest, fairest, and bestest of them all. Thou mustest take on this quest. You shall write a book that shall describe the journey of becoming a main character. This will grant you . . .

The rest of the prophecy was unreadable.

Which was odd, because he was certain he'd completed the thought on paper before his nap.

How strange.

Well, he certainly couldn't refuse to listen to whatever a mysterious prophecy said, could he?

CHAPTER 1

BECOMING
A MAIN
CHARACTER

I, Broody McHottiepants, from the bottom of my most generous and humble heart, have decided to teach you, dear reader, all of my secrets to becoming a main character. Keep reading to learn how to attain all those lovely adjectives and secure a perfect plot for yourself.

I am most certainly not writing this book because someone dared me to. That would be very petty and silly of me.

I am neither of those things.

I might be described as mysterious, dramatic, handsome, brilliant . . . but certainly never silly.

Who do you want to be?

It's a simple question, isn't it? And yet, it's a question fictional characters never get asked. Our lives are molded by all-powerful Authors. Maybe my evil ex, Blondie DeMeani, wishes she could be a bookish art school student. Too bad! She gets blonde hair, red lipstick, and a vengeance complex. Perhaps my funny, ethnically ambiguous best friend would like to be a main character and experience his own romantic plot. Alas, he's doomed to always be in the background, while I take center stage.

If only Authors would consider the wishes of their characters . . . Maybe I could even achieve my dream of starring in a series that spans seventy-seven books. That would be heaven.

Hey, Authors? Call me. Let's chat.

Anyway, because you're reading this book, I assume you want to be a main character. Excellent choice. Main characters have all the fun.

What is a main character? Well, we (as I am always a main character) are the wonderful, dynamic beings who shape stories. There's a reason it's called *Romeo and Juliet* and not *Stuff Happens in Fair Verona*. A main character like me is able to save the world or fix a dystopian society, or even get a date to prom. That last one is the hardest, to be honest.

Even if, once in a while, it's a supporting character who steals everyone's heart, odds are good that a fan's favorite character is the main one. And you know what? Anyone can be a main character. Even you.

That may come as a shock, given how . . . similar many main characters are. Don't worry about that. For now, just focus on your desire to be a main character. By the end of this book, we'll have you in tip-top main character form.

What were you before your main character life began?

Although we're focusing on your future, I suppose we can spend a few minutes discussing our pasts. Think of it as a lively discussion about our prologues—our backstories.

What was I doing before I started writing this book? Why, saving the day in a thrilling novel, of course. I star in more novels than there are stars in the sky (but not as many as there are stars in my eyes), so I'm usually very busy.

Oh. You wanted me to go even further back to reveal the secrets of my dark, mysterious past?

I'm not sure I can do that. We've only been speaking for thirty-three pages. That's not nearly enough time for a first kiss, let alone time enough to reveal all my secrets. Just know that my secret past is very secret, mysterious, and sad.

Very sad.

The saddest.

I'm sure you might have had a sad past, too, being a supporting character and all, but my past is still the saddest, because I'm me. And we know my emotions are far more important than everyone else's.

Anyway, it doesn't actually matter so much what happened to you before the life-changing moment you picked up this book. Why? Because you're now a main character! Or at least, you will be when I'm done helping you. I can see the main character potential shining in your eyes, the possibility of a great plot lighting your smile, the hope of a trilogy glowing in your . . . eyebrows?

I talk a lot about main character potential, because I firmly believe that one can sense main characters in the wild. How else would I always know how to fall in love with them?

Main characters are also called *heroes*, *lead roles*, and *protagonists*. The last one is Greek for "a person who is a pro at being really awesome and saving the day."

I think.

Look, you didn't start reading this book to learn Greek. You're reading it to unlock your main character potential. This is a journey that, like all journeys, will take you the whole book to conquer. You can't just wake up one day and announce, "I AM A MAIN CHARACTER!"

Unless it's a "first chapter wake-up." If that's the case, make sure to immediately go to the mirror and describe yourself in great detail.

Is it a first chapter wake-up? Here's a quick check: survey your surroundings. Did you wake up *just* like every other morning, but there's that feeling in the air that it's the start of a new book? Potential plot crackles around you, and you've perhaps just had a very vivid dream? This is your moment.

In a first chapter, it's essential that readers know exactly what you look like, so amble on over to the nearest mirror (or reflective pond, if you're in a fantasy novel) and describe every single freckle, lock of hair, and eyelash. Oh, and *never* forget to describe your eye color. You can learn pretty much everything you ever need to know about someone from their eye color:

Brown: The most basic eye color. Very, very rarely are my eyes this hue, but it's decent for characters who are approachable, kind, and honest.

Hazel: A more flashly sort of brown. This character is slightly less approachable and much more likely to be flirtatious.

Blue: There are a wide range of shades of blue when it comes to eyes. For example, cornflower blue eyes belong to sweet love interests who are bubbly and joyful. My shining, wild sapphire eyes show that I am intense and powerful. Many people have drowned in my eyes. Luckily for them, I have recently become a certified lifeguard, in an attempt to save more love interests from this terrible fate.

And also to use CPR as a way to sneakily kiss them.

Purple: More common in female characters, purple-eyed beauties are sensuous, romantic, and possibly a little dramatic.

Green: One of my favorite colors. A little bit mysterious, intense, and vivid. Partnered with red hair, and you're probably at least a tiny bit mischievous. If you wish to brood with an emerald gaze, I recommend dark hair.

Blue-green: Your personality is changeable, your heart fickle, your beauty constant.

Black: Ooh, you're a very, very intense dude. Possibly a villain. Most certainly not a girl. Eyes this intense can only be for a male character.

Red: There's a high chance you're a supernatural creature. Also, you probably have fangs.

Gold: Dramatic, definitely a magical being, possibly a good guy. Lower chance of fangs than the red eyes.

Cat-eyed: Some characters actually have cat eyes. No, I'm not sure why no other characters find this alarming, especially if said character isn't a magical being. I'm also not sure it's a color, but I thought I should include it. I'll bring you some catnip, should we ever meet.

Gray: A great eye color because it could be magical or just very rare and swoony. It does double duty! Great for maintaining your air of mystery.

Almond: Uh, look. No. Just don't do that. Don't describe people like food, got it? (Unless it's me, and I'm your hunky ice cream mountain of a man.)

What color will my eyes be? Only you can decide. Crack out your most gemstone-like, sparkly crayons and get coloring!

Now that you've determined what your eye color says about your main character personality, you're ready for the next step. Just follow me on the dangerous roads I will lead you down, practice your steely gaze, and adopt the smirk of your choice (cruel, sardonic, teasing), and we'll be good to go.

Main characters are, in essence, the best of the best. The ones with the most adjectives. The ones on the covers of the books. They're like the Olympic athletes of plot. The Chosen Ones and the Royalty and the Vampires (who may or may not sparkle), and ... pretty much every Halloween costume you've ever worn.

But Broody, you exclaim nervously, *what if I'm a girl? I thought girls could only be love interests ... And are love interests ever allowed to be main characters?*

Well, that is an interesting point. Sometimes, yes. Love interests *can* be main characters. (And sometimes, my love interest isn't a girl.) As this book is all about teaching you how to unlock your main character potential, it stands to reason that anyone who reads it can become one.

'Cause I'm perfect, and that means I'm a perfect teacher.

Let's just go forward with some ground rules, shall we?

Me: Broody. The most perfect, most magical, bestest main character ever. I'm the Professional Protagonist.

You: A supporting character of any gender who wishes to become a main character.

Your love interest: Whatever person you wish to woo. Substitute pronouns as needed.

The Other Guy: My ultimate rival. You probably have a rival, too, so let's assume "guy" is a generic term, and fits whatever you need.

Got it?

In **Chapter 4: Finding True Love**, I'll tell you all about the love interests I've met, wooed, and allowed to tag along with me while I did all the work of saving the world. However, you, dear reader, will be able to go out and find your *own* love interests, of any gender. (Please don't take any of mine, as I'm very possessive and jealous and will exhibit sexy, manly rage if you ever breathe in the direction of my love interests.) If you don't desire a love interest, that's fine, too! Just skip this chapter

So yes, anyone can be a main character. Even you!

Signs of Main Character Potential

I'll be discussing main character potential in great depth—so deep a depth it might rival the deepness of my sea-blue gaze. Everyone may have a moment or two of main character potential when they might stride forward and capture the title of protagonist.

But not everyone is aware of these moments when they occur. Opportunities may whoosh by without you even realizing it. This is probably because many main characters are so clueless, they don't realize water is wet. Which is why they need me. To explain things to them. Brood-splain, if you will.

So to start, I wanted to draw up a list of all the important traits main characters may have, as a reference guide for you to consult. If you don't have any traits on this list, that's okay. We'll keep working on it.

- **You have more adjectives than the average person.**
Everything about you is carefully described, from the way you roll your eyes to the precise color of those eyes. Your Author has spared no adjective or adverb in her efforts to describe you, and might have even used a thesaurus to find some new ones.

- **People often tell you things you already know.**
This is a burden that every main character must bear without a single eye roll or exasperated sigh.
But Broody, what do you mean?
Let's say it's the second week of school. Unbeknownst to you, you're actually in a first chapter. You'll probably notice this soon enough when your best friend runs up to you and says the following: "Hi, <INSERT YOUR NAME>. Wow! I'm sure glad to see you, and I can't wait to go to our first class, math. Then we have English, where you sit next to that cute person, <NAME>. Remember how last week they flirted with you by telling you your hair smelled nice? Your <INSERT HAIR COLOR> hair is incredible, lush, and lovely today. And you have such <INSERT EYE COLOR> eyes, just like your parent, <NAME>. Oh! And don't forget that today is your birthday, and you're turning sixteen."

- **People often interact with you in crowds, conveying useful bits of plot information.**

Maybe someone shouts, "Wow! I hope no one goes to that abandoned factory full of werelemurs!" right when you're looking for your werelemur boyfriend. Or, maybe an adorable small child gives you a useful plot token, like that necklace that will eventually unlock the door to the castle. Or at least a slightly important box. In general, most of the people around you seem to only have one role in life, and that's aiding you.

- **You find yourself describing your appearance after looking at any reflective surface you find.** A lake, a mirror, the blade of your sword . . . Any surface can be used to sneak in some of those adjectives used to remind the reader of your beauty.

- **You're . . . different somehow.** Perhaps you're the only person at school with green eyes. Not only is this statistically close to impossible, but it also means you feel different from everyone around you. That's because you're probably a lost princess/half-leprechaun/Chosen One.

- **You just want to be normal.** You're a famous actress/musician/princess/ potato farmer, but you've always wondered what it would be like to be an ordinary teen. Granted, you're not curious about experiencing outbreaks of acne, bullying, or cramming for the SATs . . . Just prom and other fun normal-teen things.

- **You just want to be special.**
  You're an ordinary teen. The most ordinary teen ever. Perhaps even the only ordinary person in your whole family of famous actresses/musicians/royals/potato farmers, and you've always craved a more glamorous life. Granted, you're not curious about actually doing the hard work of acting/learning an instrument/governing a nation/planting potatoes. You just want to experience the pretty outfits and other fun celebrity things.

- **Multiple people seem to want to kiss you.**
  In the first three chapters, at least five characters have expressed interest in touching your face. You, of course, ignore their attentions, as you are only interested in someone truly beautiful, powerful, and full of main character potential touching your face.
  Someone like me. If I were just a simple, boring love interest.
  Which I certainly am not.
  But you do have a very touchable face.

- **Multiple people seem to really dislike you.**
  One person, in particular, really, really hates you, despite having never interacted with you for more than three seconds. They simply hate everything about you. They proclaim this loudly and often, so that everyone knows they are your archnemesis.

- **There's something strange about your family.**

Maybe they forbid you from eating garlic or they disappear every full moon or use embarrassingly outdated slang. Any of these traits could mean that they're actually supernatural creatures, and they've been keeping the secret from you your entire life.

You'll be mad at them for a few chapters, of course, but they had your best interests at heart. Everyone knows lies create insta-plot! And plot means main character status! (Don't worry, we'll dive deeper into plot later.)

• **You have no family.**
None. No aunts, no second cousins once removed, and absolutely no parents. You are also certain that this is completely normal, and not a sign that you're in fact the missing royal heir whose family has been looking for them for exactly the same number of years that you've been alive.

Wow. That's definitely not you, right? I mean, what would be the odds that some scrappy orphan is actually a main character . . . ?

• **You have a meaningful item of jewelry.**
Perhaps it's a locket with a photo of a woman you can't remember, but who has kind eyes. Or a ring with a magic stone. Or a bracelet that states: <YOUR NAME> IS THE CHOSEN ONE AND HEIR TO THE WHOLE KINGDOM. Whatever the item is, you'll constantly examine it and ponder its vague, impossible-to-understand meaning.

- **Open your mouth. Exhale. Did you just let out the breath you didn't know you were holding?** I knew it. Main characters are always forgetting to breathe, especially when they're talking to me.

Stick with me, and we'll have you rocking your main character look in no time. Trust me. Do you have any idea just how many protagonists I've given makeovers to? At least twice as many as there are pages in this book. I'm just glad one of my many superpowers is always knowing exactly what size a female character wears. If I buy her a dress, it always fits. That's because of two simple facts: number one, all main female characters are a "normal size," which actually means a conventionally thin size, because body diversity doesn't exist in YA fiction, and number two, I make sure to measure each of them while I'm watching them sleep. How else am I going to know they need size six glass slippers?

I'll detail specific main character styles later in the next chapter, as I'll be breaking them down into multiple categories, including love interests and Broodys. Oh, and Other Guys, but they don't really matter.

What Percentage Main Character Are You?
Here's how this quiz works. Keep going until you have to circle the word "false." Once you do, then check to see what percentage main character you are.

1. You already know your name, age, horoscope sign, Hogwarts house, eye color, and the ten best adjectives for describing your expressions.

TRUE.   FALSE. (YOU ARE 10% MAIN CHARACTER.
                               YOU BETTER READ THIS BOOK AS
                               QUICKLY AS POSSIBLE.)

2. You have at least one, but no more than three friends. Each has a distinct, and yet easily summed up personality.

TRUE.   FALSE. (YOU ARE 25% MAIN CHARACTER.
                               KEEP READING.)

3. You often find yourself narrating your life and refer to yourself in the third person in your own head, making it easier for a reader to learn your name.

TRUE.   FALSE. (YOU ARE 50% MAIN CHARACTER.
                               YOU MAY CURRENTLY BE THE BEST
                               FRIEND OF A MAIN CHARACTER.
                               WORK ON USURPING THEIR
                               NARRATIVE AND REPLACING IT
                               WITH YOUR OWN.)

4. You have a mysterious power/secret/hedgehog that you don't understand.

TRUE.   FALSE. (YOU ARE 75% MAIN CHARACTER.
                               DON'T WORRY. BY THE TIME YOU'RE
                               DONE READING THIS BOOK, YOU'LL
                               BE FULL OF SECRETS.)

5. Your name is Broody McHottiepants.

TRUE.   FALSE. (YOU ARE 90% MAIN CHARACTER.
                               WHICH IS GOOD, I GUESS.
                               BUT YOU'RE NOT ME, AND I'M
                               PERFECT, SO YOU HAVE ROOM
                               FOR IMPROVEMENT.)

NARRATIVE INTERLUDE: WHILE OUR BRAVE HERO CONTEMPLATES HIS ABS, EVIL LURKS

Broody let out a deep, voluminous, incredibly heavy sigh. How did Authors do this? Writing a book was turning out to be harder than overthrowing a dystopian regime.

Just to be sure, he told his reflection, "We've totally got this! We'll be the best Author ever, Mirror-Broody!"

He winked at his reflection. Man, once he was an Author, life would be even better. He'd have thousands more movie deals, a top spot on all social media . . . All he had to do was finish writing.

But, really, writing was awfully hard, and his hand hurt, and he was bored, and . . . And he hadn't gotten a chance to take his shirt off in at least forty pages.

Now would be a great time to go and find his comic relief friend for a game of sportsball. Maybe he could steal some amusing one-liners from his friend. The guy wouldn't mind. He never starred in a single book.

What Broody didn't notice, and, really, only an omniscient narrator could have ever noticed, was the person lurking in the shadows of the hallway, waiting for Broody to leave. Watching.

Plotting.

One might even say . . . villainously scheming.

A NOTE FROM SOMEONE WHO IS NOT A MAIN CHARACTER

A Note on POV
Written by me, Blondie DeMeani

Here's the thing, reader. Broody is clueless. Note I did not say "kinda clueless" or "a small bit absentminded."

That's because I don't have time for all those extra-cutesy words he uses. When you're a supporting character, you've got to make your limited dialogue count. Every line must be delivered as sharply as a swoosh of perfectly applied eyeliner.

So, Broody is clueless enough that he won't even notice I've snuck this paper into the notebook.

Or that I erased part of his prophecy.

But if you're reading this, you probably have a good reason to. (Ugh. Fine. That was one necessary modifier.)

So, throughout this book, I'll try to sneak in some notes on anything that Broody doesn't explain well enough. In return, you'll remember I'm not the villain of this story, no matter what he writes.

Deal?

Lesson One: POV

POV stands for point of view. In other words, this is the person who is narrating the story. Usually, they're a main character. Broody will say that they're usually his love interests, and in most books he's in, that's true. The dude's got charisma, I'll give him that.

However, that brings up a valid, important point. A book can be in your point of view, and you can still not be the mainest main character. (Oh. Fantastic. I've started to sound like him.) This is due to a problem we call "agency."

Agency

What's agency? Good question. You're probably asking because you're a character without any. Agency is the ability to make decisions that affect the story and move the plot forward. Agency is all about driving the story—like the way I drive my red-hot convertible into the school parking lot to get everyone to notice me every morning.

Still not sure what I'm talking about? Let's use Sleeping Beauty as an example. Now, there's a girl with very little agency. She's a princess (which she didn't choose to be) who gets cursed for the simple fact her parents didn't invite some lady to a party (and as a baby, she couldn't exactly say, "HEY, WITCH LADY, COME TO MY PARTY!"), and then she accidentally pricks her finger on a spinning wheel. *Bam!* She's asleep and has never made a single deliberate choice that influenced the direction of her story.

I guess I should be glad she's got an evil fairy godmother, and it's not Prince Charming's evil ex who curses her.

Now, if Sleeping Beauty had gone through a stretch of good old teenage rebellion and decided to seek out every dangerous-looking spinning wheel and deliberately pricked her finger with one—well, she'd be a girl in control.

Meanwhile, Sleeping Beauty's prince, though the dude remains nameless, has got some serious agency in the tale. (Of course.) He gets to slay dragons and decides to kiss some sleeping lady without even asking her permission first. (Classic Broody move. Always assume girls want you to kiss them.) He takes the fairy tale and he conquers it.

Ugh.

Anyway, dearest wannabe main character reading this, please, please, fight to have agency in your story. Do it for all of us supporting characters.

Okay, let's dig into POV.

Your Author will pick your POV for you, just like your high school will pick your uniform for you. (Well, at least mine always does, since I go to the most elite, possibly-full-of-dark-magic, private school ever.)

But just like a uniform, you'll find ways to customize your POV. Granted, I might scoff at your customizations, but that's because I scoff at everything.

No hard feelings, right?

Okay, so. You've got:

1ST PERSON: You, the main character, are telling the story, using words like "Me, myself, and I."

2ND PERSON: The main character, is uh, well, "you." Ugh. This is awkward. No wonder I never help main characters. This stuff's annoying.

3RD PERSON: Someone is telling the story about you but using your name instead of "I" or "me."

You've also got tenses to worry about.

PRESENT TENSE: Stuff happens to you in the story. "Blondie smiles at me as she gives me the secret of POV."

PAST TENSE: Stuff has already happened to you. "Blondie smiled at me when she gave me the secret of POV."

FUTURE TENSE: What are you? An oracle? Pssh. Don't worry about this one.

Hope this helps! Or at least lets you plot a suitable revenge!

xoxo, B

Ah. I set down my notebook for a few minutes to go and practice leaning sexily against a tree (my favorite yoga pose) and I cannot seem to recall where I left off.

Was I going to explain something?

Ah. Yeah, POV.

So, stories are written in a variety of points of view. Don't worry yourself too much about them, all right? I mean, the books I star in are rarely in my POV, and yet . . . I'm still the most memorable, coolest character.

In fact, sometimes it seems like the Author only uses my love interest's POV just so someone can describe my gorgeousness and assign me as many adjectives as possible. I'm certainly not complaining about that.

Sometimes, I get to have POV chapters in the sequel . . . or in an online-only exclusive, but it would be cool to have my own POV in the first book once in a while. Heck. My Author would probably get to have SIX movies made from her trilogy of books, and a knighthood or something. But, of course, that would involve the Author being smart enough to listen to me, with all my amazing ideas. Stupid Authors. Don't know a good thing when they see it.

Hmm . . . If you ever meet an Author, please tell them I deserve to be the POV star of every book. Also, please inform the Author that my brilliant, lustrous, blue-green turquoise eye color cannot fully be captured with only three adjectives—they require at least ten more.

CHAPTER 2

BROODY EXPLAINS IT ALL

Okay, we've highlighted several aspects of main character potential. Now, let's talk about some of the things you need to be a main character, and then we can jump into what type of main character you want to become. This will be an important choice, as it will dictate the plot that unfolds around you, regardless of the genre. (We'll be discussing genre more on page 124.)

Character Arc:

As a main character, you should have a character arc. No, not a giant boat to fill up with matching pairs of animals—that's an *ark*. An *arc* is a shape going from point A to point B to point C, like below.

See?

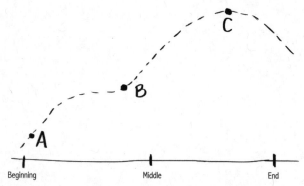

All main characters start at point A.

You know who doesn't start at point A? NON-main characters. Supporting characters.

BLONDIE DeMEANI, that's WHO.

Ahem.

Here: have a diagram of Blondie's arc.

See? No arc. No potential to be anything but an evil ex-girlfriend. Got it? I mean, I know you, dear reader, are aware that Blondie isn't a main character, but just in case she teleports into your room . . . maybe remind her of that fact?

Anyway, let's get back to talking about something much better: me. I always have a character arc. I will admit to you, fabulous reader, that I, Broody McHottiepants, begin each story as a *flawed* character.

There's nothing wrong with flaws, though. They shape us and aid us with plot. Thanks to the plot I transform from my flawed self into my absolutely perfect self, so that by the end of the book, readers are so in love with me they'll buy the sequel.

What flaws could I have?

Ordinarily, I would never share this list, but as you and I have built up a certain level of trust over the past few pages, I feel confident you won't share these with all of your friends or my enemies. (Or the characters who are both your friends and my enemies. Darn nice-villains. Always confusing.)

1. I care too much about you.
2. I don't care at all about anyone.
3. I only care about myself.
4. I ignore my emotions.
5. I ignore you.
6. I ignore basic manners, social norms, and general decent human behaviors.
7. I'm not human.
8. I'm not actually alive.

See? There are plenty of flaws for you to choose among. Also, get used to that list, because I'll need you to do all the work to help me change into a semi-decent person. As an attractive, brooding male, I simply don't have the time to devote to improving myself.

Oh, and by the way, while you're working on improving me, you're going to have to improve yourself, too.

Isn't being a main character great?

Types of Main Characters

Now that you know about character arcs and the flaws main characters need to overcome, I think we're ready to dive into various types of main characters and how they differ from one another.

There are many, many kinds of main characters in young adult fiction. I could describe them for days, but that might put you to sleep. And although I have been known to kiss many fair slumbering maidens awake (preferably without asking them if they'd like to be kissed), currently, I'm rather incapable of doing so. Paper cuts.

I know. It's a real tragedy. My kisses have been known to make knees buckle and stop hearts from beating.

For the sake of simplicity, I've broken down main character types into four categories:

1. Broodys
2. Love Interests
3. Other Guys
4. Antagonists

Broodys

If you just asked, "What's a Broody?" I'm not going to respond. Instead, I'll slink off to the dark, moody woods where I will sulk for days. The woods are a wonderful place for sulking—there are trees to hide in, like how I hide my emotions from the world, green leaves the exact color of my dazzling emerald orbs, and moss as soft and fluffy as my hair.

You've been reading this book for how long? And you can't remember what a Broody is?

But yes, I am the embodiment of all the brooding, attractive male characters in every book in the YA world. As such, I happen to know a lot about my various forms. Granted, I am devastatingly handsome in all of my incarnations, and my bright wit and broken heart are sure to win you over if my dashing smile fails to (a rare occurrence, I assure you).

Think of the below types of Broodys as various colors of the same awesome car. (Or horse, depending on your time period.) They'll all get you where you need to go (a.k.a. to a trilogy/movie deal/award-winning novel) but you can only use one model at a time. Some Broody features come standard. These include angst about my past, casual misogyny, a deep love of my own self-importance, and really nice hair.

Oh. And in the below descriptions, we're just going to assume you're my love interest. Who wouldn't want to be my love interest, right?

So many people, Broodster. Dozens, thouosands, of people aren't in love with you.

xoxo, B

Top Types of Broodys

The Contemporary, Standard Broody

Description: Sure, I just used the word *standard*, which might be interpreted as a very boring descriptive phrase for someone as incredible as me. But isn't it a good thing to have standards? Especially when it comes to your love life?

This version of me is exactly that. I'm the basic Broody model, with great hair, a blazing bright smile that could blind entire villages, and deep emotional distress I'll refuse to talk about. I'm most commonly found in high school settings. You'll recognize me because I'll be the attractive, unattainable guy at whom you won't be able to stop staring. Aside from my raging male jealousy and my incessant need to ignore everything my love interest says, all of my other traits will be filled in according to the requirements of the plot.

Most Common Swoonworthy Feature: My smirk. As a standard Broody, without a fancy outfit or cool sci-fi gear to distract you from my adjective-infused bod, you'll be inclined to stare into my shining eyes more. Since this is technically the "real world," my eye color will probably be limited to boring real colors, though as a Broody, they'll still be a rich hazelnut, and not blah boring brown.

The Historical Broody

Description: This version of me is usually a gentleman and almost always sophisticated. (Unless we're in the Wild, Wild West, and then I'll be a rough-around-the-edges cowboy.) I look dapper in a cravat, even if I'm not exactly sure what a cravat is, and I'll probably have a nice hat, too. Despite existing in a long-ago time (or the eighties . . . although certain Authors get upset when I call that Historical. No idea why.), I'll have modern mannerisms and be utterly delighted that my love interest is such an unusual girl for her era. Why, she wants to read and vote? Capital! (I'll also use random historical slang, even if it's anachronistic, because it makes me more dashing.)

Likewise, I'll be free of all common habits or vices that might shock a modern reader. I certainly won't have a snuffbox or wooden teeth. Thankfully, I'll also avoid awkward historical fashion choices like the codpiece. In short, I'm about as historically accurate as a really good Halloween costume.

Most Common Swoonworthy Feature: My incredible, adorably antiquated manners. Have you ever wanted a man to hold your carriage door open for you? Or arrange to marry you without ever speaking to you? I can do both of those things!

The Jock Broody

Description: I like sports. I'm very fit, and I'm also very popular. That's about it.

I mean, I might also throw really good parties and have a conflict with my father who has unrealistic expectations about me, but what Broody doesn't do those things?

The sport I play doesn't matter. Usually, it's football, but don't worry, there will never be an in-novel narration of any of my games, probably because my Author finds the sport incredibly boring. I may also run track or play hockey. I'm pretty sure I've never been a competitive fencer or bowler, but who knows what the future holds?

Most Common Swoonworthy Feature: My letterman's jacket. This very warm, highly coveted item will be yours one day, as the plot and weather will conspire to make sure you're shivering and I'll be uncharacteristically courteous and insist you take it. You'll secretly sleep in it, pretending that you're actually wrapped in my warm, manly arms.

The Mysterious Foreign Broody

Description: This version of me comes in two flavors:

The poorly researched, ambiguously brown Broody

I come from a foreign country that's probably made up, or might as well have been, for all the accuracy of the Author's portrayal. My skin will be described as a shade of chocolate or coffee, which will be highly offensive, but my Author will find it romantic. I'll speak perfect English, but I'll be sure to use my mother tongue (thanks, Google Translate!) for two things: swearing and terms of endearment.

Most Common Swoonworthy Feature: My complete lack of any accuracy or respect for the nationality I represent.

The British Broody

Usually, a result of my Author binge-watching far too much BBC without ever doing any actual research on the assorted cultures and traditions of Great Britain. As a British Broody, I'll be from London, because there really are no other cities in all of the UK, or maybe Scotland (that's basically a city, right?), and I'll have a dashing accent. I'll exclaim, "Bloody hell!" at least once per book, and enjoy tea, crumpets, tea cakes, and anything else involving tea, but will never ever drink coffee because coffee does not exist in England and that is a fact.

Most Common Swoonworthy Feature: My accent. Yes, it bears repeating. American readers simply cannot get enough of a British accent. We could be reading them the dictionary, and they'd still swoon.

Watch.

"Hullo, luv. Fancy a cuppa?"

You totally swooned. Admit it.

The Handsome Loner Broody

Description: I don't have any friends, and I don't want any. This will, of course, make my love interest all the more determined to become my friend. And once she learns that I have a deep, dark secret that requires me to stay away from everyone else? She'll stick to my side like Velcro. Please note: The actual secret doesn't matter. It could be that I am the last in a proud line of werelemurs, or simply that I'm allergic to pumpkin spice lattes. Whatever it is, it will attract my love interest. Secrets are like catnip to girls.

Most Common Swoonworthy Feature: My inability to trust anyone. Sure, this might not sound romantic to you right now, but I assure you it is. Just wait until I finally, finally start to lower my walls after you've spent 230 pages performing heavy emotional labor to help me with all my issues. That will be epically swoonworthy, right? Maybe we'll even spend a whole five pages on your problems.

The Guy in a Band Broody

Description: I'm in a band. It's a pretty sweet gig, especially because my tour bus is about the size of a minimall. I'll write at least one love song about my heroine, and I might even be willing to give up my fame for her. You see, I just want to be normal ... provided "normal" still includes "ridiculously attractive and also wealthy."

Most Common Swoonworthy Feature: My meaningful tattoo. My Author spent at least thirteen hours researching this tattoo, picking out its precise significance and location on my perfectly chiseled body. It will not only show just how rebellious I am, but will also be used as a plot device to convey an important part of my backstory.

The Military Broody

Description: As the leader in the rebellion/captain of the hot-royal-dude's guard/improbably young general, I'm stern, serious, and incredibly muscular. I'll probably be in charge of training you to be a better warrior, which I will do shirtless.

Everyone knows shirtless is the safest way to fight.

Most Common Swoonworthy Feature: My abs. Or my dedication to duty.

But mainly, my abs.

The Lovable Rogue Broody

Description: I break the rules. But in a really attractive way. I'm short-tempered and quick-witted, but I have a soft, melty-warm center. I've probably saved a bunch of orphans or I volunteer at an animal shelter . . . or at least I don't often push people into oncoming traffic. I'll challenge you to leave behind whatever moral code you think is right, and promise to make you "live a little." My mode of transportation is incredibly dangerous but very sexy—a motorcycle/stallion/the fastest ship in the galaxy.

Most Common Swoonworthy Feature: My quick wit, especially in the face of certain doom. Look, all Broodys are witty. I totally get that. But I'm . . . extra witty. Perhaps because I've lived such a hardscrabble life or because I'm utterly fearless, I'll be sure to make cutting, sarcastic quips, even when facing down the Evil Powers That Be.

The Paranormal Broody

Description: I'm a mythical being, and I look like a teenager . . . mostly. I'll have at least one dramatic beautiful trait that makes me different from all of those other average humans that have asked my love interest to prom. Due to my supernatural superness, there's a good chance I'm very dangerous, and an even greater chance that I am incredibly dramatic. But I'm also a great boyfriend! I'll do super-romantic things like kidnap you or turn you into an undead monster or ignore you for the entire school year before kissing you. That's because one of my magical traits is my inability to exhibit any common human decency.

Most Common Swoonworthy Feature: My eyes. Whatever color they are, you've never seen anything like them before. Often, they even have their own magical powers, which will be revealed when you gaze deep into them, like willing you to forget all the plot holes in our story.

The Princely Broody

Description: I'm a prince or duke or emperor or . . . basically any male in a position of power over a country, city, or municipality. Because of this, I'll be a bit of a womanizing jerk—Who am I kidding? I'll be a bit of a jerk no matter how much power I have—and will need a sweet protagonist like you to make me realize the error of my ways. My magnificent parties and flawless sense of style have probably bankrupted my kingdom, but you won't mind after I give you a taxpayer-funded makeover, right?

Most Common Swoonworthy Feature: Uh, did you not see the part about my incredible wealth? My castle? My impressive stable full of horses and/or unicorns?

Fine, fine. Let me also mention my GIANT WARDOBE full of pretty dresses that just happen to be in your size.

The Forbidden Broody

Description: I cannot be with you, dearest love interest, for reasons that . . . depend totally on the plot. They may range from "I'm going to die if you kiss me," all the way to "My friend doesn't like you very much." But somehow, we will find a way to be together. Granted, we, uh, might not both survive after we do get to be together . . . But that's just a minor detail, right?

Most Common Swoonworthy Feature: My ability to draw you closer in very romantic moments, and then push you away dramatically.

Common Variations:

The Broody who is your brother's best friend

The relationship is forbidden by your brother, because he and his best friend treat women horribly, and if you were to date me, your brother's best friend, you'd realize that. Granted, a better option would be for your brother to just stop treating women so poorly, but why should he have to do any work?

The Broody who is the brother of your best friend

Not to be confused with the previous category, this version of me is off limits because you'd end up spending time with me instead of your best friend. Obviously, your BFF should realize that she's never going to get much screen time, no matter what version of the story she's in, and should just let us be together.

RMAL BROODY   JOCK BROODY   PRINCELY BROODY

Love Interests

I'll give you a moment to rouse yourself from your dreamlike stupor. After assembling so many lovely, lovely Broodys in one place, it's to be expected that you'd be a bit dazed.

But now it's time to talk about female main characters. Since I am the main character, I call these my love interests, but I'd like to take a moment to remind you that every last one of you is worthy of having whatever love interest you want. Please substitute any and all pronouns in this book. Love is love.

And if you chose to have a story without a love interest, that is completely fine, too. You're always a main character, remember? Ignore anyone, and any story, that doesn't make you feel like one.

As I am the one writing, please know:

She = the love interest (Change pronouns as needed. I, for one, would like more occasions where my love interest uses he/his or they/them. Authors? Get on that.)

Me/I = Broody (Don't change a thing about me. I'm perfect.)

Anyway, let's get moving on these love interests—er, sorry—this subcategory of *main characters*.

Ordinary Love Interest

Description: She is very plain and ordinary and thinks nothing will ever happen to her. (She's wrong! I'll fall in love with her!)

Habitat: Her room, because she has no friends and/ or has strict parents. Or a punnily named coffee shop. Really, anywhere she can ponder her boringly normal existence and daydream about dating me.

Hobbies: Wishing something exciting would happen; writing in her diary about her dreams; daydreaming about me.

Defining Features: None. She's ordinary, remember?
But wait! *Because* she doesn't have any self-esteem, I bet she'll fall madly in love with me if I tell her she's beautiful. This will be easy to do, because although the Ordinary Love Interest assures everyone via her narration that she's ordinary and plain, she'll also be thin (perhaps even willowy) or maybe curvy (but, you know, only socially acceptable curvy), with long eyelashes framing bright eyes, and a button nose that will be adorned with a small smattering of freckles. The rest of her skin will be flawless.

Ordinary-But-Actually-Magical Love Interest

Description: She always thought she was ordinary . . . well, aside from never knowing her birth parents/ that strange event that happened to her when she was a child/her incredibly vivid dreams. But now, after a single kiss from me, she knows she isn't.

Habitat: A creepy, small town or New York City. All paranormal roads lead to New York City.

Hobbies: Stumbling into a secret paranormal world she had no idea existed; wondering about her birth parents' identities; being clumsy; being secretly more powerful than anyone else at whatever magic exists in her world.

Defining Features: Abnormally colored eyes, usually in the shade of a gemstone. Possibly wings or pointed ears or pointed teeth or pointed . . . toes?

Not-Like-Other-Girls Love Interest

Description: This girl loves stuff that *no* other girl does. Like cool music. And board games. And roller skating. She's *so* original that she simply can't stand any other girl because they could never understand her. But I can. Granted, I'll choose *not* to understand her for at least the first five chapters, but that's just for the sake of our plot.

Never say I'm not generous.

Habitat: Someplace other girls don't hang out. No, not the men's bathroom. Think a skate park or a record store. Wherever it is, she makes sure there are absolutely no other girls there, even if she has to lock them in the previously mentioned men's bathroom. Because she's not like other girls.

Hobbies: Judging other girls; being into stuff she assumes other girls don't like.

Defining Features: She's tough. She's tiny (remember, love interests are never tall), but she's tough. She probably has a band tee or two, but cuts it in a sexy way to show you she's still a girl.

Manic Pixie Dream Girl Love Interest

Description: Ah yes, the manic pixie dream girl. I know her well. She has taught me how to live my life many times, what with her vintage dresses, quirky date ideas, and silly phrases that make no sense if you actually think about them. Her life goal is to fulfill all of a male character's emotional needs while managing to have absolutely no character arc of her own.

Habitat: Wherever I need her most.

Hobbies: Fixing my life, being quirky, singing. She *loves* singing. And dancing. Usually in places where singing and dancing should not occur, like funeral homes and the principal's office.

Defining Features: Neon bright hair or some sort of 1950s style. Bright eyes. A constant, bubbly giggle. More pep to her step than every other character combined.

Strong Female Character Love Interest

Description: The Strong Female Character is here to kick butt and take names. But she's also, you know, here to fall in love with me, revealing her soft, squishy side. There's no battle she can't win, unless it's one where she gets knocked unconscious and I, as male hero, have to save her.

Habitat: The practice ring of her badass sport/form of combat.

Hobbies: Fighting people, arguing, flashing her eyes dangerously, hiding her deepest feelings.

Defining Features: Surprisingly, she has almost no muscle definition, despite her incredible strength. If she has a scar, it's small, and in no way detracts from her overall beauty.

The Bookish, Writerly, In-No-Way-a-Version-of-the-Author Love Interest

Description: She's pretty, but doesn't know it. She'll have a few physical attributes she really dislikes and will complain about them often, whether they're her hips or her nose. Oddly enough, these are the same features that the Author dislikes about herself. (Hey, Author? Are you listening? You're beautiful, just the way you are. And I'm not just saying that so you'll write me a sequel.)

Habitat: The library. All love interests love libraries, but this one really adores them. She might even work there, or at a bookstore. There's always one book she's absolutely in love with. At least she is, until she meets me. Then she's in love with me.

Hobbies: Uh, reading and writing, duh. And more artistic pursuits such as painting or music. If there's modern technology in the book, she'll certainly be a book blogger and take more Bookstagram photos than the rest of the Internet.

Her other hobby, of course, is arguing with her parents. That's because they don't want her to be a writer/ballerina/other artistic pursuit. They'll lecture her with the exact same doubts and fears that swirl in the Author's head. Therefore, when The Bookish, Writerly, In-No-Way-a-Version-of-the-Author Love Interest triumphs, finds love with me, and wins at her art, well, it's the Author's win, too.

Defining Features: Often, her hair is pulled back in a bun and secured with a pencil for extra writerly points. Of course, she'll have glasses, too, so that when I, in all my Broody wonderfulness, remove them and free her hair from the bun, not only will she be more conventionally beautiful, but she'll barely be able to see me, making me even more glorious to behold.

The Other Guys

These guys are the absolute worst. If you're one of these characters, please do me a favor and leave any story we share, okay? I know love triangles are good to create tension in the plot, but I'd prefer my rivals to be incredibly bland and very easy to beat.

Anyway, here are the typical rivals I might have in a story.

As always, here's my note on what the descriptions refer to. Honestly, you're so lucky to have such a kind, giving, incredibly swoonworthy dude writing this book for you. Could you imagine if a different, lesser, fictional character archetype wrote it for you?

In the "Other Guys" section, we'll assume that "you" is you, dear reader, who is clearly deeply in love with me, Broody.

The Nice Guy Next Door

Description: You've known him forever, but never *noticed* him before the story began. He's different now. He's attractive and has manners and gets along with your parents. *(Yuck.)* As far as physical features go, he should be the total opposite of whatever guy you're currently crushing on. (Hint: me.) So, for example, if your current man has tattoos, jet-black hair, and an onyx-eyed stare that could melt rocks,

The Nice Guy Next Door will sport nerdy T-shirts, a shaggy blond mane, and quirky glasses that hide his sweet, forest green eyes.

Usual Broody Rival: Any of them.

Threat Level: Uh, did you not see the part where I describe him as having manners? This guy is so low on my risk radar, I might even befriend him.

The Friend Who Moved Away but Now He's Back

Description: Do you remember that little boy you used to play with in the sandbox? Maybe you promised to marry him when you grew up? No?

Don't worry. There will be at least one flashback scene to help you recall the exact moment. You haven't seen him in ten years, but he'll reappear just as your novel begins.

Usual Broody Rival: Historical Broody (if a marriage proposal was discussed) or Contemporary Broody.

Please note that if this friend left suddenly, and then became a wildly successful rock star who secretly writes a song about you . . . yeah, that's actually me. No Other Guy could do something so frustratingly vague and also incredibly romantic.

Threat Level: Moderate. Those fictional promises of marriage exchanged between toddlers are really hard to break.

That Kid in the Orphanage with You

Description: This kid grew up with you in whatever overly dramatic, pre-first chapter situation you find yourself in. Perhaps it was truly an orphanage, or maybe it was a bleak dystopian boarding school but, regardless, he understands you because of all you've been through together.

Usual Broody Rival: Princely Broody.

Threat Level: Low. He's in love with you, yes, but he's more in love with dramatic statements against authority. He will begrudgingly come to your royal wedding, or he might sacrifice himself in the epic last battle just to get out of seeing you with your fated love.

My Best Friend

Description: He's almost as attractive as me, and therefore almost as popular as me. But he's, well . . . nicer than me. He's the one who explains to you that I skipped your violin recital because it was secretly the third anniversary of my pet rock's disappearance, and I was too emotional to attend. He'll also actually take the time to get to know you and your personality, which we know I am far too busy to do.

But, I'd just like to point out that as he is my best friend, he's a very, very supporting character, and nowhere near the protagonist I am. Why would I befriend anyone who might rival me in main character magicalness?

Usual Broody Rival: Lovable Rogue Broody. We have a long-standing history of betting and gambling on everything, so of course we might gamble over my love interest's heart.

Threat Level: Non-existent in Book One. But be warned: this is the type of creeping cute guy, hidden Broody who can completely take over a sequel.

Your (Male) Best Friend

Description: Similar to the Nice Guy Next Door, but whinier and less helpful. He doesn't like me because he's threatened by how good-looking I am. Your parents (if they're not kidnapped/turned into newts/disappeared) probably like him a whole lot. But when has a parental figure ever been correct in a YA novel?
Answer: Never.

Usual Broody Rival: Paranormal Broody. He exists as a contrast to my supernatural self. Where I have gleaming fangs and spun-silver hair, he has braces and a messy mob of brown hair. Only one of us will risk your life multiple times throughout the novel. Pretty sure it's an easy choice who you'll pick.

Threat Level: Very low. However, he'll be the favorite of some very vocal fans.

That Nerdy, Awkward Guy You Know

Description: He's not your best friend, and he doesn't live next door, but as you're a main female character, he's bound to be interested in you. Unlike me, he never skips class/magic lessons/tutoring sessions, and you can count on him to always be able to fill you in with boring backstory.

Usual Broody Rival: The Handsome Loner. Sure, that Nerdy Guy will help you with your homework, but will he get you grounded after an exciting first date involving skipping class and tearing off on my motorcycle?
    Didn't think so.

Threat Level: Moderate. He reads books, and we all know love interests *love* books.

Special Case Scenarios
As you may have noticed, most of these rivals are about as threatening to me as a feather duster. While I am loathe to admit it, that's not always the case. Sometimes, even I can be out-brooded. This rare occurrence, like an eclipse of the sun, may be

beautiful to watch, but could also scar your vision if you stare too closely. It usually occurs in sequels, where the Author needs to up the brooding factor and cannot make the first version of me any broodier. I'll discuss sequels more in **Chapter 8: You're a Main Character . . . Now What?**, but for now, here are some examples of the "rival with brooding tendencies."

The Former Villain

Sure, he was trying to kill everyone in the first book, but now he's reluctantly working with the good guys to fight the Big Bad. Why? Well, maybe he has a crush on the love interest.

This is very, *very* bad for an ordinary Broody. It's a well-known fact that the more dangerous I am, and the darker my backstory is, the more my fans will adore me.

And what could be more dangerous than a villain? Someone who actually got the narrative freedom to do bad stuff? Plus, a tragic backstory of being evil *until* the power of true love changes him. Yikes. That's scary good brooding material.

This phenomenon can also happen in movies (more about movies, a.k.a. books made of pictures, on page 307), when the actor chosen to play the villain is more attractive than the hero.

My Older Brother

Sigh. He's cooler than me, has a sweeter ride than me, and is edgier than me. How on earth can I compete? Even worse, as my brother, we will have similar quests. For example, to rid the world of our evil father, we will have to work together, even as I watch him steal my love interest away from me. This is, in part, due to main character attraction being a genetic trait. If I had five brothers, all of them would be madly in love with the love interest, too. Heck, even my second cousins and third cousins once removed have fallen for her.

My Mentor

Not my bearded, old Merlin-esque mentor. I would never be worried about being in a love triangle with that guy. The other type of mentor. The young, hot one, with rakish good looks and a brilliant smile. He's dangerous—even more dangerous than I am, if you can believe it—and love interests desire nothing more than danger. Seriously, if it weren't for us hunky men, all the world's love interests would be playing dodgeball on roller skates in the middle of busy highways.

The hot mentor may manifest as my vampire sire. (Note: Do not call him a vampire daddy. That makes him far less attractive and makes me feel very uncomfortable.) He's the person who made me into a vampire and is therefore older, sexier, and more dangerous than me. You should be seeing a theme by now.

A Completely Unexpected, Mysterious Character

These guys sometimes appear, and stun *everyone*. Even I've fallen in love with them before. I cannot even describe them because they're so magical and appear so suddenly. Just picture everything you've ever wanted in a fictional character, and *bam*, that's him.

He'll be able to solve plot problems with just a wink, and can communicate like a Nice Guy Next Door, while moping like me. . . . He probably even has a motorcycle. Ugh. Let's stop talking about him.

A Note On Ensemble Casts:

Once in a while, you are enjoying a perfectly lovely story, when you realize something. There are . . . *other* main characters in your book with complete character arcs and love interests and kissing scenes . . .

Before you throw a temper tantrum and quit the story, take a deep breath. Sometimes, stories have more than one protagonist. Often, this is known as an "ensemble cast" story, which is a fancy French word for a type of pastry with many layers. I think.

Should you find yourself in an ensemble story, simply proceed as if you are the only main character that matters, and you'll be fine.

Antagonists

Ah, yes. There is one more category of main characters. I saved the best for last. And by best, I mean worst. Antagonists. That's Greek for "a person who causes great agony to very good-looking heroes." I sincerely hope, dearest reader, it is not your goal to become one of these shady, dangerous, world-domination-seeking characters, and you will simply use the following guide as a way to identify them and stay far, far away.

Every story needs a bad guy, so the antagonist is, unfortunately, as unavoidable as a dramatic makeover scene is to a "Cinderella" retelling. I hope your antagonist is someone easily defeated.

Or something. You see, unlike the other types of characters, sometimes antagonists don't have to be people.

No, I don't mean that they're all centaurs, giant squids, and fairies, although they certainly can be. But the main force opposing me and my goals (er, and yours, too . . . Your goals are exactly the same as mine, right?) can be anything from a particularly angry storm cloud to a man with storm-cloud-gray eyes.

The distinguishing feature of antagonists is their opposition to the heroes of the story. If it weren't for the bad guys, my brooding stories would be very short. . . .

So maybe, upon reflection, I should actually be thankful for my antagonists? Hmm.

Well. Why not? I am, after all, the most generous and wonderful main character to have ever existed in the history of time. I suppose I can find room in my heart to write a little love letter to the antagonists of my novels. So, without further ado:

Dear Antagonist,

Thank you so much for your single-minded determination to ruin my life. Your passion, focus, and dedication to causing misery is so impressive that I wonder if you've ever had a moment to yourself for fun. Well, besides that time you cackled evilly from the tower of your castle of doom.

Your motives are often vague, your backstory hastily sketched, and your goals rather futile. And yet, you've never let that stop you from attempting to take over the world/ruin prom/get me to date you. That's dedication right there. Good for you.

And thank you, too, for giving me so many opportunities to look positively dashing during our battles. It was so kind of you to never attack me while I was delivering a particularly witty one-liner. I owe you a great deal of gratitude for having that one easily exploited weakness, which allowed me to defeat you right before the end of the book.

Thank you again, and best of luck with the whole "world domination" thing.

xoxo, Broody

There. My generosity truly knows no bounds. What other hero would be so kind as to thank the person who's opposed him in countless books? Surely not that other guy in the love triangle. He'd never be so unexpectedly nice, right?

And I am truly the gift that keeps on giving, because I'll now share with you a rundown of many of the most common antagonists, just in case you should run into one. Please feel free to take notes. You never know when you'll encounter an antagonist. They don't all show up with a magnificent cape and an echoing, evil laugh.

Things Out to Ruin Your Life, a Short List

Bad People: Self-explanatory. These people include my parents, mean teachers, mean friends, and my evil ex-girlfriend. There's not a lot of reason why they're so mean. Perhaps their socks are too tight. Or maybe they had too much love in their childhood

(because we know that having too little love from your evil-overlord father results in . . . me!)

I'll break this category down into just a few more, because there are tons of evil people in stories, and I don't want you to get confused.

Evil Overlords: The baddest of the bad, and therefore the ones given the least characterization. These guys (and, let's be honest, they're usually men) are out to conquer the city/world/universe and will do anything to achieve that goal. They're very powerful, often wear black or red, and tend to live in massive, well-guarded fortresses. They also really love kidnapping love interests, even if it would make more sense for them to just destroy everything instead of meddling in your romantic life.

Evil Rich People: Not quite as hell-bent on world domination, these antagonists are often found in dystopian or contemporary novels. They have a lot of power and would like to have more. Your plot puts you directly in the way of them achieving their goals, so they'll have to use their money to try and ruin you.

Bad Teachers: These teachers aren't in your school to educate you or help you pass the SATs. They're there to cause drama and make plot happen. Maybe they assign an impossible homework problem or make you work with your nemesis. Whatever their aim, it seems incredibly vindictive toward you. That's okay, because they're just cementing your main character status by allowing you to overcome their cruelty.

Annoying People Interested in Preserving Their Rules: These bad guys show up most often in paranormal stories, but sometimes in historical or fantasies. Here's an example: Let's say you're dating me, and I'm a sexy supernatural being. You are an average mortal teen, who finds it thrilling to go to prom with a werelemur. However! There are laws against werelemurs dating ordinary humans. I was so busy brooding about the impending full moon, which brings with it the urge to climb trees and other lemurish things, that I forgot to mention those pesky laws. So, now our romantic prom will be broken up by the supernatural fun police.

Annoying People in Positions of Power: They're not necessarily evil, but these people—mayors, CEOs, bankers, headmasters, etc.—want you to conform to whatever their rules are. Of course, you're way too cool for rules, so you'll rebel.

Evil, Evil, Ex-Girlfriends: My ex-girlfriends are always evil. They hate you for dating me, because once that happens, they . . . uh . . . have nothing to do except plot revenge? Yeah. Pretty sure that's it.

A NOTE FROM SOMEONE WHO IS NOT A BROODY

AHEM.

Okay. Let's see if Broody rereads this before he publishes this joke of a book. I'm betting my brand-new designer purse that he won't.

Look. I get it. I'm the "evil" ex, because how could I be anything else? A toxic blend of jealousy, internalized misogyny (yeah, I'm not as stupid as I look), and desire to make Broody look good in comparison has me doomed.

Here's the thing: there's a real problem with our stories. It's all good if the attractive guy is confident and ambitious, but Author Forbid we ever have a heroine who strides on to page one and knows just how badass she truly is.

For whatever reason, perfectly applied eyeliner is not a skill that is recognized as being worthy of anyone but a being of pure evil. Oh, sure the heroine can get a makeover halfway through the book and still be good. But if she starts her character journey with contouring applied so perfectly she could stop traffic with her cheekbones?

She might as well have "Super Evil Lady" written on her forehead.

And that's not fair. Not at all.

xoxo, B

Antagonists, Continued

Nice, Well-Meaning People: These folks actually want to help you. The problem is that their idea of helping isn't actually all that helpful. Perhaps your parents want you to focus on your studies and have decided that your gorgeous, brooding, possibly-a-vampire boyfriend is not exactly helpful in keeping up your GPA. Instead of having a civil conversation with your charming boyfriend where they'd learn he's an excellent history tutor as he's really three hundred years old, they forbid you from ever seeing him again.

Misunderstandings: Let's have a moment of silence for my dear, dear, dead Great-Great-Great Uncle Romeo, who was slain by this very antagonist. In his honor, I promise to also jump to conclusions instantly, never research, nor pause to communicate with my love interest, before charging ahead based on a rumor.

Time: Oh, this cruel, cruel monster. It is impossible to race against. It runs out so quickly. Heck, it could probably win any race ever. Annoyingly, Time has never shown any weakness in the face of me batting my obscenely long eyelashes and has never once agreed to grant me an extension.

My Feelings: Woe to the main character who must face this foe!

What a mighty, powerful, full of might and made of power antagonist this is. You see, although I love you deeply, we simply cannot be together.

For . . . reasons.

I'm sure you understand.

Just remember. It's not me. It's you.

Er . . . I mean, it's not either of us.

Of course not. You are perfect, and I am even more perfect.

I just also have a very dark, secretively held secret that I can't tell you . . . for two hundred more pages. (But! You can take the quiz a couple pages ahead and learn your own main character secret.)

Your Feelings: Perhaps you suddenly feel guilty for ditching all of your former friends to spend a romantic evening with me, or you suddenly wonder if dating a werelemur when you're allergic to fur is actually a good idea. You'll use your feelings as a shield against your *truest* feelings, which are, of course, ones of undying love for me.

Myself: In addition to my actual feelings, I am very good at doing things to make your life more difficult. But I *swear* it's never my fault. I mean, getting brainwashed and turning into a villain happens to tons of people, right? It's almost as common as a thunderstorm!

And if I decided to date my evil ex again

YEAH RIGHT

it's only for some complex, plot-related reason that I can't tell you about yet. Or if I forgot to pick you up for a date, I was simply doing something more important. Like styling my hair. Regardless, I assure you, whatever cruel things I've done, I had a very good reason.

Vague Bad Things: These can include bad weather, impending nuclear destruction, and the flu. Anything that tries to keep me away from you, dearest love interest. Indeed, there always seems to be an impressive number of things trying to keep us apart. One almost wonders if the Author is just trying to bolster a weak page count.

Pop quiz!

What's your favorite type of music?

1. Jazz
2. Classical
3. Showtunes!
4. It's really obscure. You've never heard of them.
5. Country Music
6.
7. Rock and Roll/punk rock/metal/something loud and angry
8. Pop—especially that song that everyone hates, and yet gets stuck in their heads

Which of these are you most likely to drink in the morning?

1. A latte
2. Blood . . . er. . . blood orange juice
3. The milk in my cereal bowl
4. Organic, fair trade coffee from a coffee shop you've never heard of
5. Tea
6.
7. Coffee as black as my soul
8. The most evil Frappuccino ever created

Which of these would you pick for your next vacation?

1. An elegant, quiet, and yet charmingly simple location. Like my parents' chateau in France.
2. Someplace cold and dreary like my mood
3. Disneyland!
4. I could tell you, but you've never even heard of the location, so why should I bother?
5. Skiing with my bff, like we have every winter!
6.
7. Ugh. I dunno. Some big city where I can get lost in the crowd.
8. Cheer camp

you could turn into any bird, what would it be?

A magnificent, and yet understated, snowy owl

A bat—er . . . I mean a bat-like bird. Yes. That.

A butterfly!

A *Setophaga chrysoparia* [formerly *Dendroica chrysoparia*], which is a rare and endangered bird species, more commonly known as the golden-cheeked warbler. I don't expect you to know that, of course. Or to care about it. Or to care about me.

A robin, which is oddly enough, also my best friend's name

7. A hawk soaring above the land it used to love, looking for danger

8. A peacock, but pink

If you chose . . .

Mostly 1s: Your secret is that you're actually incredibly wealthy. Why you're keeping this a secret and not buying your love interest a pony and a prom dress, I don't know.

Mostly 2s: Okay, Count Obvious. You can count on one hand how many chapters it will take your love interest to guess your secret: that you are actually a terrifying, immortal being.
Don't worry. That won't put any sort of a damper on your relationship.

Mostly 3s: You . . . don't have a secret. I'm sorry. You're just too bubbly and kind and lovely to have secrets. Maybe attempt to find a werelemur to bite you so you can acquire a secret?

Mostly 4s: Hmm. Let me guess. I couldn't possibly understand your secret, could I? Yeah, right. Your secret is that you are a jerk. Luckily for you, your love interest will have never heard of the words "respectful, considerate relationship." (I mean, neither have I, but at least I like good music.)

Mostly 5s: Your secret is that your best friend is in love with you. Yes, I know technically this doesn't count as your own secret, but it certainly will add a lot of drama.

Mostly 6s: Wow. You're really good at this. You're so secretive even I don't know what you want.

Mostly 7s: I get it. You had a terrible thing happen to you in your past, and now you're a rebel.

Me, too, dude. Me. Too. Wanna start a band together?

Mostly 8s: Hah! I caught you, Blondie. Trying to take this quiz, huh? Tough luck. You don't have any secrets.

SPECIAL NOTE:

Characters Who Are Sometimes Evil

This might be a little confusing to you, since you are a brand-new main character who's never been in a story before. But in addition to your standard evil characters, there are some characters who are only evil occasionally. We can call them part-time antagonists.

Some people might call them *antiheroes* but I prefer to reserve the use of the word *hero* for myself alone, thank you very much.

These part-time antagonists are often roughly the same age as us. Perhaps they are the children of evil overlords or your greatest rivals. They will try to foil your plans, as any evil character would, but sometimes the part-time antagonist will do nice things for you, too.

They may even become your love interest. In that case, please refer to earlier sections as well as the next section of the book. (Again, look at me being helpful! Don't I truly deserve to star in everything ever?)

The Sliding Scale of Evil/Attractive

You might have noticed in my enormously clear and helpful main character breakdown, a simple fact: sometimes, the line between the actual villain of a story and the Broody is very thin.

Surprised? You should be. Many main characters are shocked to learn their love interests are actually slightly evil. Very, very attractive villains with excellent backstories are often actually a version of one of the Broodys mentioned above.

IS THAT CUTE PERSON ACTUALLY A VILLAIN OR A LOVE INTEREST?

Where did you first see this person?

1. At school. They got lost, and I helped them find their way.
2. At school. They gave me the wrong directions to class.
3. In a dream. I saw a flash of their beautiful face and cannot forget it.
4. They tried to arrest me.
5. After trying (and failing) to befriend me, they tripped me in a hallway.

Describe this person's smile:

1. Innocent and joyful, as if they had swallowed a thousand butterflies.
2. Like the chipped and broken plastic knife you find at the bottom of a bag of takeout food.
3. I've never seen them smile, but I can only imagine that it would be as brilliant as the first light of dawn.

4. They have a smile that is cold and brilliant, and yet does not reach their eyes.

5. They smirk, smirkily, and fold their arms in a self-satisfied matter, contentedly.

What was the last thing this person said to you?

1. "Wow! I've never met anyone like you."

2. "You smell like feet."

3. <INSERT MYSTERIOUS QUOTATION WHISPERED TO YOU IN A DREAM HERE.>

4. "You are going to destroy everything!"

5. "Just wait until I tell my father."

If you took this person on a date, where would you go?

1. Probably someplace romantic.

2. A picnic on a cliff, so they could push me off it.

3. We'd spend a perfect evening together, where every moment passes like a beautiful, expertly polished jewel. The specifics don't matter.

4. We'd sword fight/verbally spar/duel with magic, and the victor would buy the loser ice cream.

5. A date with *them*? Ugh.

If this person were a dog, what breed would they be?

1. A corgi! Cute and tiny and oh so adorable.

2. Something with fleas. And possibly rabies.

3. The most magnificent, sleek, graceful greyhound ever.

4. A half-wolf half-husky hybrid, with icy blue eyes.

5. A cat. They don't play by the rules.

If you chose . . .

Mostly 1s: There's no way this person is a villain. I'm sure they're a great character, but you've got to know there's not an evil bone in their adorable body, right?

Mostly 2s: Definitely evil. Definitely not romantic.

Mostly 3s: So, you haven't actually *met* this character yet, have you? Maybe reserve judgment on if they're evil or not until you meet?

Mostly 4s: Well, they are certainly an antagonist . . . but methinks there's a chance for love to blossom.

Mostly 5s: This person sounds like an absolute jerk. I bet all your fans will try to claim you two love each other deeply, but don't worry, it will never actually happen in the books.

Let's face it. Evil is sexy. But only to a point. There's a seesaw of evil and sexy. I call it the Seesaw of Evil and Sexy. I'm very clever. No one will ever find the evil overlord attractive, with his greasy black hair and his sneer. But what about his henchman? That one who helped the heroes just once, demonstrating a slight waver in his dedication to bringing about the end of the world? Yeah. He could be a Broody. You never know.

But why is this the case? I suppose because there's very little a female main character likes doing more than saving/improving a male character's life. And who better to improve than someone who just needs to be shown the error of his ways?

This is a rare instance where you cannot flip male and female main characters. No main male character has any desire to actually improve an evil female character, although he might seduce her for plot reasons. Actually, now that I think about it, none of my favorite relationship things work if you flip roles. How strange.

Ah, well. That's probably because girls are just better at improving guys, you know? They're just so wonderful, girls, with all their fainting-at-the-most-dramatic moments, and changing every priority so their lives revolve around the guys they just met . . .

I mean, it would be *much* harder to be a main character if I couldn't expect that bland, supportive girls would drop everything to cater to my every need and desire.

Wow, Broody. You're getting pretty deep there. Be careful you don't think too hard and short-circuit what little brains you have. What's even stranger is that all of these dynamics seem to be between a guy and a girl in stories. There is more to the world than a relationship. And even if we are only talking about relationships, there are plenty that don't involve a guy and a girl. Sure, I might be evil, but I know a lot about love. Getting dumped in chapter three in every book does that to a girl. I mean, really, Authors? Can't you . . . I dunno . . . try harder? Give us main characters a little variety in the roles we're playing? Make our fictional worlds reflect the real lives of your readers a little more?

~~I mean, does the world really need another story about some bland, boring, rich dude saving some~~

Ahem. This is me, Broody, again. I apologize for the above. *Someone,* actually *stole* my beautiful notebook to write that strange, strange paragraph above. Don't they understand that I have many, many emotions which can only be helped by having a female character dedicate her life to me? I don't have time to run around *helping* other characters. I'm writing this book for them. Isn't that enough?

Other Characters

Look, the book is called *Brooding YA Hero: Becoming a Main Character (Almost) as Awesome as Me,* not *Being Content as a Supporting Character.* Are you sure you want to even waste brain cells learning about other characters that exist in my world?

Yes?

Okay. Fine. But I warned you.

Here are some other characters you may find in my books: As a reminder—because you probably need one. Main Characters get reminded of stuff all the time. Especially at the start of a sequel—in the below definitions, "me" refers to your favorite, most magnificent, magnanimous guide, Broody McHottiepants.

Your Quirky Best Friend

She's odd, she's funny (at least to your Author, so you'll have to laugh at her jokes), and she'll probably dislike me.

Your Sassy Minority Friend

Pick a minority, any minority! This character should be crafted solely out of clichés seen on TV and involve absolutely no research. Also, she might die, you know, to further the main character's plot. Sorry.

The Guy Who Lives Next Door to You

He's got the opposite hair color to me, never smirks, and is very, very helpful. But he might be too much "like a brother" for you. Keep an eye on this dude. He might turn into a rival of mine at any moment.

The Suspiciously Attractive Other Guy You Talk To

I just don't trust this guy. He's really good-looking, and his personality is multidimensional, and . . . Wait! Is he on the *cover* of the sequel???

All Other Guys

Okay, after those last two, I think it's time for me to do something I excel at: hasty generalizations. Let's just assume every single dude who has ever spoken to you is a potential rival of mine, got it?

Your Parents:

They won't like me—that is, if they're even alive. Luckily, they will also be incredibly busy with their own goals, jobs, and other elements of their lives so they won't notice all of the plot-related adventures you and your love interest are having.

Additional tips about the parents (and remember, the more charming and wonderful they are, the more likely the plot will . . . uh . . . *remove* them, so try not to get too attached):

- *Your Mom:* Usually overworked, doesn't do enough mothering.

- *Your Stepmom:* Evil. Very pretty or thinks she is. Insults the Love Interest every chance she gets.

- *Your Dad:* The perfect mix of clueless and unobservant.

Your Older Brother, Who I am Friends With

He's cool. I hang out with him a bunch, but he won't like it when I start dating you, because he knows that he'll disappear from the narrative. He probably doesn't like you that much, but that's because he's a super-cool guy who doesn't have time for anything but sportsball and dude stuff.

Your Precocious Small Sibling

This one will like me. They'll have an adorable kid-like way of speaking, too. Also, they'll be oddly perceptive and will out your secret at the worst possible moment, but so cute, you can't stay angry for long. (Unlike real life.)

The Cruel Teacher

Wants you to fail, despite your best efforts to succeed.

The Kind Teacher

Wants you to succeed, despite your best efforts to drop out.

The Wise Old Mentor

Some old, usually cranky person who wants to teach you about stuff in a possibly unorthodox manner. You'll get attached to them, which is a problem because they always die.

Broody's Edgy, Even More Attractive Older Brother

He's like me, only more attractive, and more dangerous. Often shows up in sequels and second seasons.

My Father

Hates me.

My Current Girlfriend

Hates my love interest. Wears makeup and high heels, signaling that she is clearly evil.

My Jokester Best Friend
The comic relief. Also, maybe a minority! 'Cause that's cool! (As long as they're supporting roles only.)

The Popular Girls
Pretty, vain, and cruel. Oftentimes unintelligent. Always rich. Never nice, because no ambitious girls are nice. Duh.

The Popular Guys
Handsome, sexually active, and stupid. Usually play sportsball.

A Brief Note on . . . Blandness

Dear reader, I must confess something to you. As you can tell from all these character descriptions, sometimes my favorite worlds of fiction suffer from something I can only call . . . blandness.

It is a sad thing to admit, but yes, we fictional characters can only be as diverse, multifaceted, and unique as our writers make us. So, please, if you have a chance to write stories, consider your characters, and please make us less bland. We don't want to be vanilla ice cream. We want to be a complex sundae of delicious things, to reflect the incredibleness that is the real world.

xoxo, B

NARRATIVE INTERLUDE: WHILE OUR WISE HERO WANDERS, EVIL PONDERS

Broody looked down at his notebook. He certainly hadn't written that last section. So who had?

He had only taken a brief break in the hall to stare meaningfully at the crowd of New Girl characters milling around, waiting to be drafted into new novels. Broody believed it was important to spend time making eye contact with each of them, so they had that *insta-recognition* that always sparked true love.

He always found it funny that what Authors called *insta-love* was usually just him and the exact same love interest he'd been matched with in the last story hitting it off immediately.

Authors were so strange.

But while Broody had been busy with the good work of ensuring a love story would blossom, someone had clearly crept into his room and written that note criticizing the blandness of main characters.

How oddly, unexpectedly dangerously, unexpected.

Broody didn't mind being bland. He was very good at it. Vanilla ice cream with sprinkles on top: that was how he liked to think of himself. The sprinkles added just a tiny bit of flair to his basic, vanilla character traits. The sprinkles, like the adjectives, made him cooler.

Who would ever dislike that?

Sure, Broody knew there were many, many characters who only got to be in a few books, but that wasn't *his* fault. And, after all, he was writing this book to help! So any characters could become main characters, provided they followed his very specific approach.

He was determined to figure out the mystery of who had tampered with his manuscript. After all, this opus was his only ticket to getting back to a starring role in books! If it had been hijacked by a rogue character, why, his very existence was at stake!

Wait. "At stake?" he mused, repeating his interior monologue out loud. "Stake?"

Was this . . . a plot?

Absolutely not. He shook his head, letting his tousled mane tousle even more. He didn't have time for some silly little missing notebook plot.

He was meant for greater things. Like taking main characters to prom, or writing a number one chart-topping love song.

Better to resolve this quickly, so he could get back to his usual stories.

And so he departed on a walk through New Story City, asking each archetype he met if they recognized the handwriting.

Unexpectedly, he found that each time he approached a group of character archetypes, they wanted to know what he was writing. And so, he told them. And that always led to a discussion, in which each character started giving his or her own opinion about what it meant to be the main character.

Baffled by this strange phenomenon Broody rubbed his face as if to rub away his baffling bafflement. But it only succeeded in making him more perplexed, which was almost the same as baffled, but a slightly deeper sort of confusion.

All fictional characters are highly trained to recognize the small nuances among related emotions like that. He thought about rereading the earlier pages of his book to see if there were any clues, but that seemed like an awful lot of work. So, instead, he kept asking other characters in the hopes that repetition would suddenly yield a plot twist.

And it seemed to Broody that all characters had a lot of opinions on what should be included in a main character's journey.

"Don't forget about the plot!" a mentor-type called.

"Discuss how important love interests are!" a matchmaker cried.

Some characters thought it was strange that Broody didn't know who had written in his book. A few suggested his evil twin, or another case of brainwashing. But what was written was such an unbroody-like thought, it couldn't have possibly been him. Even his evil twin would agree that no one related to, inspired by, or cloned from a Broody could have possibly written the strange note.

"Will the best friend get any screen time?" Broody's own best friend asked.

"Well, you can now, I guess," Broody told him, jotting down their exchange, which was more than his best friend often got dialogue-wise. "Unless you've got something funny to say? You know I'm not very funny."

"No, I'm not your comic relief friend. He's over by the water fountain." Broody's best friend's voice was sad, and he spoke in a sad manner, shaking his head sadly.

Broody frowned at his own interior monologue. He sounded rather . . . blandly repetitious, even to his own ears.

Could that note have been right?

No.

Impossible.

He wasn't boring! He was Broody McHottiepants . . .

And he wasn't allowed to star in any more books.

"Hey, dude, wait," Broody called, catching his friend before he walked away. "Quick question to help me out with the next chapter. What do I have that you don't?"

"Are you really asking me that?"

"Uh, yeah." Broody repeated the question.

Broody's best friend sighed. "I don't know. Just about everything? You get the girl, the plot, the medal. Heck, sometimes you don't even need friends to accomplish your goal. And me? All I get is a couple witty lines, or I get kidnapped and possibly tortured. It's not fun."

Broody furrowed his brow. It was a noble brow, even when furrowed, although Broody didn't quite know what that meant. He assumed it had something to do with him having the forehead of a prince, but a very handsome one, and not one of those weird inbred ones from the Middle Ages. Habsburgs—that's what they were called. He could remember that because they'd been discussing them in a history class where a love interest had been present, so he'd paid attention to impress her. Plus, he enjoyed brushing up on his history; he never knew when he'd be written into a historical novel.

Why, one time, when he'd been playing the prince of an undisclosed European nation in the 1600s . . .

"Uh. Broody?" his best friend asked. "You know, it's rude to start having a flashback memory when you've asked someone for advice."

"Oh, right. Sorry." Broody blinked his brilliant, beautiful, bright blue eyes. That was a fabulously alliterative sentence, he realized, and congratulated himself. He was truly becoming a better writer by the minute.

The best friend sighed. "I guess, to me, being a main character means you get to have a whole story about you. Not a novella, or one episode where the writer magnanimously lets you save the day. A *whole* story. That's all I want, really." Broody's best friend glanced at the crowd around them. "That's all any of us want, I suppose."

"Why, then, you should be more like me!" Broody announced, giving his friend a high five. "Thank you for your help. I'm off to finish my book! You should totally buy it when it comes out. It'll be in all the stores!"

In a rush, Broody hurried back to his room, ignoring how the town had already shifted into some bleak dystopian village, with small concrete huts, all in depressing shades of gray. The setting changed as new stories were drafted by Authors. It was something all the characters were used to by now.

Although he did hate the obnoxious overhead sirens and robotic voices that always came with the dystopian. He much preferred the peace and relative quiet of the generic suburbia setting. Plus, suburbia came with way better coffee.

Broody returned to his desk, excited by what he planned to write next. That was just like a great best friend: giving him all the useful ideas, and asking for absolutely nothing, not even credit, in return. Broody loved having supporting characters as friends.

They were just so . . . supportive.

If Broody had been paying more attention, though, he would have realized a faint scent of strawberry lip gloss lingered in the air.

For someone *was* reading and editing his book.

Someone downright . . .

Evil.

CHAPTER 3

HOW WILL YOU ACHIEVE MAIN CHARACTER STATUS?

So, now that I've introduced myself, and we've discovered who you are, how will you truly achieve your main character status? That's what you want, right? Or do you secretly wish to remain a supporting character who will only appear in a few chapters and never receive any beautiful fan art of yourself?

Yeah, I didn't think so.

After the last chapter, I feel confident that you have the main character appearance down, so the next step is to get you inside a story. A bunch of main characters sitting around, talking and flirting with one another does not a story make. Although, once in a while, my intense gaze and flirty eyelashes can fool my readers into thinking that's all they need in their books.

As we discussed, you'll never be quite as magically wonderful as me, but that's okay. No one is. That's why I'm Broody McHottiepants, ten-thousand-time gold medalist in the Love Triangle Marathon.

You know who's never won a single love triangle? Blondie DeMeani.

#

For a story to be a story, nine out of ten Authors recommend something called *plot*. The tenth Author is a literary fiction writer who believes beauty and story can be found in stream of consciousness narrative, so we can ignore her opinion.

The plot is simply the stuff that fills the gaps between kissing scenes. At least in any book I've ever been in. Are there books without kissing? This is worth exploring.

But you'll need more than plot to be a main character. You have to have setting! Genre! Tension! And so many other elements that'll get mixed into the creative batter of your novel. It takes more than just a pretty face to make a bestselling, main character-driven tale, my friend.

However, these features can be confusing to new main characters, such as yourself. After all, secondary characters exist on the page barely long enough to piece together what the plot could possibly be. They might not even know what a plot is.

Good thing I'm here to help.

Truly, I should receive an award for my generosity. Or, at the very least, a hug. Which is actually an award for both of us, because my hugs can alter your very heartbeat to synchronize with mine. And who doesn't want a matching heartbeat? That's at least five levels cooler than matching friendship bracelets.

As I was saying, I am the picture of generosity. Have you ever met a main character so intent on helping the less fortunate characters of the world? I didn't think so. Just remember that when you start to think the Nice Guy Next Door is a better choice for you, all right? Or when I do something cruel and coldhearted, like breaking up with you because it's a Tuesday.

In fact, allow me to present to you this "Broody Gets Out of Bad Character Jail Free" card I made myself as a reward for my own generosity and kindness in writing this book for you. Should I ever do anything unkind, like ignore you in front of my popular friends, simply look down at this coupon tucked into your purse and remember that I am, by far, the most wonderful fictional boyfriend ever.

Wow. This whole "being a kind of nice guy" thing is really appealing. I mean, I get presents, I get your never-ending adoration, I get book deals . . . What's not to love? Maybe I should do something else that's nice.

Okay. Not only am I going to do a nice thing, I'm going to use it to help explain what makes a story compelling.

What follows is a closely guarded secret. It's been handed down for ages. I can trust you, dear reader, can't I? We've been through so many pages together already. Surely you won't betray me and give this secret to an antagonist, or worse, to my romantic rival?

All right, here it is . . .

THE BROODING YA HERO CHOCOLATE CHIP COOKIE RECIPE

Ingredients
- 1 box cake mix, any flavor, the kind you'd use to make cupcakes for my birthday, which no one ever remembers (Except you. You won't forget, right?)
- ½ cup butter or margarine, softened the way my heart softens around you
- 1 tablespoon milk, roughly the same shade as my usual skin tone
- 2 teaspoons vanilla, 'cause the blandest of flavors is perfect for my bland love
- 1 egg, preferably a dragon's egg that you risked your life to retrieve, but a chicken's egg will work, too

Optional Goodies, a.k.a. "Characters"
(Pick one or two. These are not ensemble cast cookies.)
- ½ cup chopped nuts
- 1 cup semisweet chocolate chips
- 1 cup white chocolate chips
- 1 cup butterscotch chips
- A handful of M&M's
- Raisins
- Craisins
- Braisins (probably not a real thing, but they should be)

Instructions

Heat oven to 350°F (325°F for any pans darker than the dark secret I'm currently keeping).

In large bowl, beat cake mix, butter, milk, vanilla, and egg with electric mixer on medium speed until smooth, or mix with spoon. (Bonus points if you dance like you're at prom with me while doing so.)

Mix in additional 1 tablespoon milk if dough is too dry. Stir in goodies. Keep dancing.

Drop dough by tablespoonfuls, spacing 2 inches apart on ungreased cookie sheets.

Bake cookies 10 to 12 minutes or until edges are set. (Centers will be soft and cookies will be very light in color.) This is probably enough time to read a chapter of an excellent book featuring me.

Cool 1 minute; remove from cookie sheets to cooling rack. Remind yourself that you're always cool, because you have the secret to Broody's cookie recipe.

Right, so now that you've made those cookies, and presumably are mailing me some, let's talk about all the things they represent.

The cake mix is the setting. No one invents a setting completely from scratch, right? I mean, I suppose you could rename *trees* into *Shxsas* and break all the laws of physics in a made-up world, but that sounds like a lot of work. It's much more fun to start with a familiar setting, like "a small town high school" or "outer space" and make it your own.

The goodies? Yeah, those are your characters. The story changes with whatever you mix into it. A cookie with chocolate chips and raisins is going to taste a lot different from a cookie with butterscotch chips and craisins.

And the plot? That's the egg and vanilla and butter—all those good things that make the magic happen. Cookie dough is delicious, it is true. But you know what's not delicious? Flour and whatever else is in plain old cake mix. You need the egg and butter to make it yummy, just like a story with a pretty setting and cool characters isn't yummy without plot. This magical ingredient in a story holds the elements together and, in turn, that's what holds a reader's interest. With a good enough plot, why, you'll charm the reader into staying up all night with you, until they turn the last page, bleary-eyed and as hungry for more blood—er, books—as any vampire.

We've already talked a lot about the characters, and even though I'd love to tell you more about myself—it's my favorite topic—my coauthor is threatening to cut some of my beautiful adjectives if I keep babbling. So, regretfully, I must stop talking about me and resume our discussion of the other elements essential to attaining your main character destiny. Sorry, but I'll do anything to keep that fifteenth time my eyes are referred to as emerald orbs of pure light. I'm sure you understand.

Setting/Genre

I've combined setting and genre because I feel it's hard to talk about one without the other. I've woken up in Victorian London countless times, but sometimes I wake up to find vampires, and other times, it's steampunk clockwork monsters chasing me. So, take it from me as a main character, you need to immediately identify your genre and setting, or risk having a rogue monster mar your perfect skin.

If I have to describe them separately (and I do because my coauthor is making me), I'd say *setting* is the window to the soul—no, wait, sorry, those are my eyes. Setting is what the reader would see if they peered through an actual window of the book. The landscape, the buildings, the way the sunlight glints off my bronze skin . . .

But setting is more than that. It includes the foods the characters eat (I prefer manly foods like steak, and patriarchy pie), the types of music they listen to (manly music . . . like whatever '80s songs my Author listened to as a teen), and the way they speak (manly—you know, accompanied by grunts, and arm waving and eyebrow waggling).

Genre, meanwhile, is the flavor of the story—the rules of the game. Almost all stories pick one genre, and marry it, like a good love interest and her hero. There's no law against genre hopping, so yes, you could have zombies attack your high school and battle them off with Excalibur and then escape into outer space . . . but that's a lot of work. As a main character, it's hard enough thinking of witty one-liners in the face of danger. Save yourself some effort, and stick with one genre.

My fictional character passport is full of stamps from the countless genres and worlds I've been in, and as a seasoned (and altruistic) traveler, I've graciously decided to pass on some of that knowledge and experience to you. The following could save your life one day, so pay attention and read carefully!

###

Come On Over to Contemporary!

This is the default genre for many of us fictional characters. In this world, teenagers, often called "students," attend an oppressive, boring place called "high school." They jostle for position at "lunch tables," play "sportsball," and daydream about a strange, magical ritual dance known as "prom."

On the plus side, in contemporary fiction, the laws of gravity, and of common sense, are pretty much as one would expect them to be. No mysterious UFOs or rabid unicorns crashing your party. Even so, the Author will turn the "dial of coincidence" all the way to its highest setting. (One might even say they'll turn the dial to 11. Because what's a story written for teens without a pop culture reference from over thirty years ago?) So, if you ever meet someone in a crowded airport in chapter one, you can bet they'll be sitting next to you on the plane and flying to your final destination. Some might call this creepy. I prefer to call it true love.

Packing List:

- Your phone. This will never actually be used to solve any plot-related issues, but it will cause a lot of trouble for you when it breaks or you miss important calls.

- Your car. Every main character in contemporary YA must be at least sixteen and have a vehicle of some type. Luckily, there are no silly rules limiting teen driving to certain hours, and all of us main characters pass our driving tests instantly. We also all have cars that perfectly match our personalities. That guy next door has to drive his parents' old minivan. Me? I have an obscure, expensive sports car my Author found for me on Pinterest.

- A quirky T-shirt. What better way is there to show off your sense of humor than a T-shirt? Your Author wisely chose your wardrobe, knowing that a T-shirt will never go out of style, no matter how many years it took her to write your book.

- Coffee of some sort. All contemporary main characters need caffeine. The drink is exactly whatever your Author drinks, whether it's a complex latte or straight black, no sugar. No, I'm not sure why you have the spending habits and caffeine addiction of a middle-aged adult, either.

Fall into a Fantasy!

This is a magical place (literally), and it's full of excitement. It's also full of vaguely feudal European references, which are poorly researched. Oh, and there's always tons of white people. Usually, there's a map in the front of your book, and you're gonna need it, 'cause there are tons of countries. How else is the Author going to arrange marriages between royal heirs?

If you're a main character in a fantasy, odds are you're either the recognized heir to the kingdom, a lost heir, or someone who will save the kingdom and marry into the royal family. So, in short, life in a lush castle is in your future.

Which is good, 'cause usually your life before the first chapter kinda sucks. You're probably an orphan, or your only relative might die immediately before your plot starts. A lot of people die in fantasy. Try not to get too attached to anyone, not even your love interest, and especially not that kindhearted mentor you have.

Unless he's also your love interest. Then it's okay to kiss him.

Other helpful hints for fantasy: Pay attention anytime there's a prophecy. It's probably about you. If there's a Chosen One, yup, that's you, too. Also, whatever magic exists in your world, you'll probably be the absolute best at it. At the very least, you should be able to use it to solve about 87 percent of your problems.

If you're a girl in a fantasy novel, be sure to announce loudly how you just want to have adventures and sword fights, and declare your hatred for needlepoint often. It is a simple fact that any female character in a patriarchy-based fantasy novel who actually enjoys needlepoint will not be a heroine. It's almost like we demean women who enjoy activities typically coded as feminine. Weird.

Packing List:

- A sword. A bow and arrows may be useful, too, but a sword is a must. You'll learn how to use it in a very short training montage, and don't worry, you'll never gain any ugly muscles from the practice.

- A horse. These creatures are basically cars with legs, and are capable of galloping across the land with no need to rest or to refuel. Unlike in real life, where horses require actual effort to maintain.

- A tool with which to do magic. It can be a book or a wand or a particularly nice rock. The magic system you're using will never be explained in depth, so don't worry too much about it.

- A meaningful . . . thing. A tattoo? An earring? A toenail clipping? Whatever it is, you've had it since birth. It's secretly very powerful, and it will save your life at the exact moment your Author realized she had no idea how to do so without it.

- The patriarchy. Sorry, you can't escape it, even in a fantasy world.

Spend a Day in a Dystopian!

A dystopian world is . . . well, it's actually probably Earth in the future. (But *shhh!* Act *shocked* when you realize that, because it's a big-deal reveal for the reader every time.) There's likely been some sort of disaster that has made the world divide into Sections. (Capitalization is *very* important in dystopian worlds.)

Technology in a dystopia is a mixed bag. Sometimes you'll be fighting the evil, oppressive overlord with just a bow and arrows. Other times, you'll have cool, sci-fi-ish tech.

The good news is that no matter how oppressive the government is, they always provide proper dental care for all of the citizens they squash beneath their dictatorial feet.

Packing List:

- An object to represent your Section. Make sure it's something easy to visualize, so someone can make an online quiz called "What Section Are You?" to determine their significance in the world.

- A makeup bag. Don't worry. Whether you're running for your life or fighting to survive in an inhospitable climate, or even just napping, your makeup will never smear.

- An object from the Time Before. This little thing will reveal, to the surprise of the reader, that the story is not actually set on a distant planet, but on Earth! Of course, if they'd read the back of your book, they'd know that already.

- A book on military strategy. You'll be expected to be an expert, despite having no leadership experience, so you'd better read up.

Have Fun in a Historical Novel

A little similar to a fantasy, in a historical novel you'll find more pretty girls in dresses, more witty men in waistcoats, and more masquerade balls. In fact, Masquerade-flu is a rapidly spreading disease that has infected many genres, but I digress.

If you're not wearing a corset or a waistcoat, that's okay. Historical does span a wide range of time, like the entirety of mankind's existence up until the present day. So you could find yourself in ancient Rome or be a 1960s flower child.

But wait, Broody, you say in a panic. *I don't know how to live like an ancient Roman! And I don't want to sweat in the uncomfortable polyester they wore in the '60s.* Don't worry. Think of historical fiction as *The Past! The Theme Park Version!*

Sure, you may have to eat some weird food, like mutton, or you might have to wear one of those aforementioned corsets—and if you do, you will faint, but it won't, like, permanently break your rib cage or cause any lasting harm, so don't worry—but most of what you experience will be almost modern day. Slang might even still sound more like contemporary speech than anything else.

Packing List:

- A maid. I mean, who else is going to help you into those elaborate dresses and style your delicate pile of curls, leaving one to twist artfully against the porcelain arch of your neck? Not me, that's for sure.

- Deodorant and toothpaste. Everyone (except the villain) will have great hygiene in this historical world.

- A list of characters' names. There are a lot of people in this type of story. If you forget to pack it, don't worry. There's often one tucked in the back of your book.

- Your modern sensibilities. These are an absolute *must*. All main characters in historical novels are easily identified by their modern, twenty-first-century opinions on relationships, politics, and social justice. If you're not an anachronistically outspoken woman, you're certainly not a protagonist.

Subgroups:

Time Travel

If you were to mix a fantasy with a historical novel, you might end up with a time travel (or steampunk, but let's focus on the former). In a time travel, nine times out of ten, it will be a love story between a person from modern times and their historical love interest.

Sometimes, the love interest will even be a historical figure, so it's a bit like kissing your world history textbook. Sexy!

As a general warning, these romances are often . . . complicated, as long-distance dating often is. Either your love interest will die, decide to remain in their true historical time period, or venture to yours. Good thing you don't need any sort of ID to survive in the modern world.

Of course, it's far more common that you'll spend tons of time falling for this historical hottie, only to return to your own time, and fall in love with his reincarnation.

Not that I'm bitter about being replaced. Why would I be bitter about being replaced by some modern guy who looks just like me except with better hair and cool modern clothes and probably a much better chance of not dying of cholera. *Ugh*. Not fair.

Packing List:

- A list of rules about time travel. They're never the same in any two books. Can you travel to meet your past or future self? Better check the rule book!

- A textbook. There's going to be a lot of name-dropping, because all famous people in the same decade hung out at the exact same spot.

- Your wealth. After all, no one wants to time travel to a distant past to fall in love with a serf busy farming turnips for a living.

Retelling

These are pretty cool. They can contain parts of any of these other genres, but their main magic is their twist on a familiar tale. It's "Little Red Riding Hood" *on motorcycles*. It's "Cinderella" *during the Irish Potato Famine*.

The story your Author retells will provide a framework for your tale. But don't worry. In this world, no one will have ever heard of the original. Even if you happen to be reading the very same Shakespeare story in your English class, no one will ever question that your narrative is eerily familiar. No, not even your friend Mercutio, who's probably wondering why his name is so weird.

Dear reader, one piece of advice. If you're dating a guy named Romeo, maybe try and get your families to start getting along before you or your boyfriend of, like, fifteen minutes run off and do something reckless, okay?

Packing List:

- Sorry. You've got to be so oblivious to the source material that I can't recommend anything; it might give a vital clue away. I mean, what if you're in a "Rapunzel" retelling and I recommend you bring a hairbrush? Way too risky.

Help! You're in a Horror

Eep. Horror stories are not a happy place for me. Not at all. This genre is *dangerous*. Often, half of the romantic couple, no matter how happy they are, doesn't survive to the end. And I don't know about you, but I don't like those odds. These books will feature very scary things, and not in the secretly-a-very-sexy-fictional-boyfriend sort of way. Danger will lurk around every corner. There will be blood splatters everywhere. On the floor, on your face, even on the cover of your book.

As usual, the adults will be clueless. Unlike usual, the adults may actually be chainsaw-wielding bad guys.

I prefer the adults who don't notice that their daughter is dating a vampire, to be honest.

Packing List:

- A flashlight. Essential, even though you'll lose it when something drops from the shadows.

- A warm sweatshirt. It's guaranteed you'll be fleeing something in inclement weather.

- Please leave your sense of self-preservation at home. You should have absolutely no common sense. Always call out, "Who's there?" to that mysterious creepy voice or even go investigate . . . instead of *running away*.

Time for a Thriller or Mix It with a Mystery

A thriller is kinda like a horror, but less gory. For example, if you get a panicked phone call from your cousin who says that werelemurs have eaten half the school (and none of them morph into handsome men ready to date you), well, that's a horror. If you receive a phone call that something bad is going to happen to your pet lemur, and you have to follow the obscure clues that could just as easily be someone's trash to track down the person who called before Lulu the Lemur gets hurt? That's a mystery. If you're on a quest to save Lulu the Lemur, all while trying to avoid the gunmen intent on ending you for reasons that will not become apparent until the final fifty pages of the book, then you're in a thriller.

Confused by the difference between thrillers and mysteries? So is your Author. Mysteries usually involve using "clues" and "deduction" and being far nosier than is generally good for you, to track down information, all while avoiding "red herrings" (which are not actually fish, usually) and compiling your list of "suspects," before having a "breakthrough" and cracking the case. Sometimes you even get to wear a cool hat and carry around a magnifying glass. Thrillers are like mysteries, with extra bonus danger. And lots of explosions.

Though mysteries and thrillers are usually set in the real world, they're barely related to the contemporary genre, because despite being a high schooler, you'll have all the spare time you need to investigate murders, disappearances, and other things that the cops probably don't want meddling kids involved in.

Packing List:

- Vengeance. It can't hurt to have a strong motive for revenge in these stories.

- A notepad. For writing down clues about the mystery, even though the culprit is actually someone you'll meet in the first three chapters.

Partake in a Paranormal!

It's just like contemporary, except your love interest is a hundred-year-old magical creature who loves dating high schoolers. The setting is, again, an average high school, almost always located in either a boring, small town where nothing ever happens, or New York City, where everything happens, but you're not allowed to attend because you have overprotective parents.

There will be a complex backstory certain to unfold over a number of sequels. Multiple love interests will be introduced throughout the series, and the magic rules will keep expanding to fill any emerging plot holes. You will probably find out that you are the absolutely most special of all the special supernatural beings. However, your internal narration will still remind us every page or so about how average you are. Sadly, self-esteem is not one of the magical powers you'll ever acquire.

Packing List:

- I can't tell you what to pack. You need to be completely and utterly clueless so that your supernatural love interest can sweep you off your feet.

Sci-Fi (or . . . Space: The Final Format)

Ah yes, the space opera. I remember when my Author first told me about this strange genre. I assumed I would be singing about planets to an adoring audience. Instead, I was suddenly the captain of a spaceship, or a space pirate, or a space prince. Really, think of the coolest thing you could be, and add *space* to it. Works every time.

In these types of books, there will be epic battles and lots of countries—er—planets—for you to travel among.

If your Author's favorite thing is *Star Wars*, the scientific content will be limited, and no one will have any idea how anything in your universe works. That's okay, because it will look very cool. On the other hand, if your Author loves something else that begins with *Star* and ends with another four letter word, there will probably be some science and logic in the technology used. If your Author loves *Doctor Who* . . . just be prepared for anything. And . . . run!

Packing List:

- Some sort of cool space weapon. Something with lasers. Don't worry about how it works.

- A spaceship (duh). Again, don't worry about how it works.

- A relic of home, as you haven't seen it in a long, long time.

- A sassy robot friend.

What Genre Do You Belong In?

As a main character, it's very important to know which genre your book is. Nothing's worse than expecting to help save the world from a cruel dystopian overlord only to realize you're actually headed to prom. Totally different dress code! (Usually. I have overthrown dystopian overlords while dressed in my best tuxedo, but that's not too common. And dry cleaning afterward is expensive!)

So, here's a quick quiz to determine just which kind of novel you're in right now.

1. It's the first page of the first chapter. Where are you?

    A. Starting my first day of school, hoping the popular kids won't make fun of me.

    B. In an orphanage, dreaming about something vaguely related to the plot.

    C. Listening to a supporting character explain why our world is classified into Groups with Meaningful Capital Letters, while avoiding going to the Place that Groups Cannot Go.

    D. Starting my first day of school, hoping that the mysterious person with flashing eyes that I saw in the prologue will appear again.

    E. Stress-eating while I stare at my computer.

2. Your best friend is . . .

   A. Someone I've just met who promises to show me around school.

   B. No one. I know no one. I have no memories. Just a PLOT ITEM that reminds me of my past.

   C. Currently worried she and I will be sorted into opposite Groups with Meaningful Capital Letters.

   D. I don't have a best friend yet, but the guy with the flashing eyes has a buddy who might become my friend. Maybe. Unless they're already dating . . . and then she'll hate me.

   E. On the Internet.

3. What are you wearing?

   A. Hand-me-down clothes that aren't cool enough for the cool kids.

   B. Rags. The orphanage has kicked me out, and I only have these tattered castoffs to wear, though I dream of ball gowns.

   C. A jumpsuit, the same color as everyone else in my Group. It is not like the Time Before when people wore non-jumpsuits.

   D. Something vintage, because I totally love old things, like the guy with the flashing eyes who's actually 1,000 years old.

   E. Yoga pants and an old T-shirt.

4. What are you most afraid of?

    A. Not ever being cool enough to be considered cool by the cool kids.

    B. The evil overlord who haunts my dreams in a vaguely threatening way.

    C. Nothing. I lead a hard life living so close to the Place that Groups Cannot Go, and I am therefore fearless.

    D. The love between me and the guy with flashing eyes turning star-crossed like Romeo and Juliet's.

    E. Deadlines . . . and proofreaders . . . and reviewers . . .

5. Which of these scenarios is the most romantic?

    A. Being asked to prom by the coolest guy in school, who gives me a dress in exactly my size.

    B. Being asked to the masquerade ball by the handsomest prince in the world, who gifts me a gown in exactly my size.

    C. Holding hands while running for our lives, and magically managing not to trip.

    D. Turning into a supernatural creature to spend eternity with someone I've just met.

    E. Receiving a movie deal that turns a trilogy into four movies.

6. How old are you?

   A. A teenager, duh.

   B. Exactly the same age as the missing princess, who I am absolutely sure is not me.

   C. Old enough to be Chosen to complete the Important Task that our government tasks us with at the Important Age.

   D. About a thousand years younger than my boyfriend.

   E. A lot older than a teen.

If you chose mostly As:
Congrats! You're in a contemporary novel. You might be the new kid now, but in two hundred short pages, you will have completed your character arc, developed a personality, and maybe even been crowned prom royalty.

If you chose mostly Bs:
Sound the trumpets! You're in a uh . . .
Hang on. Quick. Here's three true or false questions. Please answer these as well.

You've seen a living, fire-breathing dragon recently.
  True
  False

Someone you know has bought a love potion . . . and it worked!
  True
  False

You're in a city that is *not* London.
  True
  False

If you've answered more **falses:**
You're in a historical novel. You might think you're only a lonesome orphan, but you're actually the missing princess! How surprising, really. You'd

think orphanages would be better at noticing how you and the princess have the exact same birthday and meaningful heirloom.

If you've answered more **trues:**
You're in a fantasy novel. You might think you're only a lonesome orphan, but you're actually the missing Chosen One! How surprising, really. You'd think orphanages would be better at noticing how you and the Chosen One had the exact same birthday and meaningful heirloom.

If you chose mostly Cs:
Stay alert, stay alive. You're in a dystopian novel. The future may be bleak, but your love and refusal of Things with Meaningful Capitalization just may save the world.

If you chose mostly Ds:
Try not to swoon, but you're in a paranormal novel. That mysterious stranger is destined to fall in love with you, and you're destined to spend at least three books mired deep in a complex plot. But your love will never fail . . . unless it's a cliff-hanger ending.

If you chose mostly Es:
Let's be honest. You're a writer, aren't you? Stop procrastinating with quizzes and get back to work. Your main characters need you!

Plot

It's time to talk about your plot. As I explained above, this is the vehicle of the story—the part where things actually happen. A plot can exist in any genre, and your Author might even combine more than one in the same book. Crazy Authors. Always trying new things. As long as they keep me blandly beautiful and full of the powers of the patriarchy, I can't complain too much.

Here are some common plots to watch out for:

Beating the Bad Guy
A bad guy/lady/government/dragon exists, and the main character(s) must use their abilities to defeat the evil.

The evil power can be anything from my evil ex-girlfriend and her cheerleading squad to a personification of death and chaos (who also might be my ex-girlfriend). We, as main characters, want to stop this evil power from doing this even more evil thing because . . . well, reasons. Look, in these types of stories, the "why" doesn't matter nearly as much as the "how" we defeat them.

And as for how we defeat them? Well, the answer is "as stylishly and dramatically as possible."

I prefer explosions, whenever possible.

Turning into Something Pretty

The main character is something plain and ordinary, like an orphan or a freshman. Through the power of plot, she is transformed into something wonderful, like princess or prom queen. The lesson of the story is that true beauty is on the inside, which would make more sense if I was madly in love with the main female character before she changed her personality and appearance to become more wealthy, attractive, or appealing.

Looking for Something Pretty

There's an object that is very pretty and main characters want to possess it. (Surprisingly, no, we aren't talking about me.) Instead, let's say it's a . . . trophy! You know, for a contest that has very vague rules. Whatever this trophy/object/thing is, the main character must absolutely find it, or else something dire might happen.

These objects are often referred to as McGuffins. Perhaps they're distant relatives of the McHottiepantses.

Solving a Mystery

Similar to the "looking for something pretty" plot above, except the something everyone's looking for is probably a murderer or a dead body (and therefore not very pretty at all).

Road Trip!
A journey, not in search of an object or a criminal, but for something more conceptual like "a meaningful sense of self" or "a life purpose" or "a hot date to prom." This trip will involve at least three wrong turns, something breaking, and getting lost. The route clearly symbolizes how there is no straight path through the future. (Wow. Did you hear how deep I just got right there? I am truly magnificent. Please, plan a road trip to meet me and sit at my feet, where you may marvel at my wisdom.)

Note: There may not be actual roads on this trip.

Attempting to Not Die
Bad things are happening and you are trying very hard to stay alive. These bad things, like acid rain or zombies or *death bombs from outer space,* cannot be defeated like the Bad Guys in other books. The only objective is survival.

This plot also works when you're abandoned on a desert isle.

But not a dessert isle. That would just involve a lot of scrumptious food almost as sweet as my boyish smile.

Comedy

Funny stuff happens. A comedy plot can be combined with any of the above plots. In general, this
type of book should be told by a particularly quirky
narrator, or one with an overinflated sense of self-
worth. I have no idea where you might find such
a character. I, for one, would never be so egotisti-
cal to call myself overinflated. I am inflated exactly
the perfect amount, and my ego is the absolute best
one I could possibly have.

Tragedy

Sad stuff happens. It doesn't get better for the characters. You'll make the reader cry, yes, but they'll
know that going into the book, because the cover
will be very dark and depressing, perhaps in a shade
of blue or black like my cold, cold heart.

Now that you know more about plot, setting, and genre, it's time for a little game:

wake up to the sound of _____, which is how I wake
                          (a noise)

p every morning. But today, something is different. I

ap out of bed, pausing only to describe myself as I gaze

ito the mirror—yup, still have _____ hair and _____
                                (color)   (gemstone)

res, plus exactly _____ freckles—and then I look out
                   (number)

ie window.

Wow! Outside I see _____
                   (mythological animal/historical figure/

____.
anet)

I can't believe it! Quickly, I dress in my _____
                                            (type of clothing)

id make sure to include the _____ that all teenagers
                            (jewelry item)

ear here. I completely forgot that today was _____
                                              (holiday/

_____. But seeing that sight outside
ipitalized verb/ day of the week)

iy window reminded me that today, I must _____ a
                                          (verb)

_____ for the first time.
(noun)

I run outside, ready to meet my destiny!

However, just as I was about to _____to my _____
                                 (verb)   (common

_____, I'm stopped by a _____.
cation)   (noise)

Something has gone terribly wrong.

See how easy that was, dear reader? Look at you, not even halfway done with this book and already starting your own story! I'm so proud of me. For being a great teacher, a talented instructor, and an amazing writer.

Sure, I'm proud of you, too, but let's focus on what's important: me.

NARRATIVE INTERLUDE: WHILE OUR HANDSOME HERO BEFRIENDS, EVIL BEHAVES

The pen scratched against the paper as Broody worked hard to record all of his thoughts, scribbling away, completely clueless that he was being watched.

Blondie watched, amazed that he had enough thoughts to string together into sentences. Perhaps he was writing a list of his favorite adjectives.

Again.

Since she'd snuck in a few times to read his progress (or lack of) on his book, she considered herself a bit of an expert on its contents. This was, of course, all part of her evil plan.

It wasn't a cruel plan. But as an antagonist, she knew all her plans would be labeled evil. Heck, after being trapped in countless "Snow White" retellings, Blondie couldn't even offer a main female character some apple juice without getting hit with the word "witch."

Or something that rhymed with that word.

Which actually hurt. Even if she was the fairest in the land, she still had feelings.

"There." Broody slammed his hand on the table. "I wrote the most incredible novel, the most awe-inspiring book on how to become a main character."

She leaned over and flipped through the pages. "Broody, this . . . This is only 156 pages."

"No it's not!" he snapped defensively, wishing he could stuff all the pages down his shirt to keep them safe. "I spent lots of time on that! Like . . . an hour, at least." If he included snack breaks. Way more time than he'd ever spent on homework.

Then again, he usually had a very pretty, smart love interest who did his homework for him. "Hmm." He thoughtfully rubbed his chin, pondering deep thoughts in a thoughtful manner. "Okay, well, I just need to go find a shy new girl or someone who needs a makeover. Then she can write the rest of the book for me, and I'll take all the credit."

Blondie glared at him. "That's not what love is."

"How do you know?" he replied. "We only dated because you liked my hair."

"Fine, if you're such an expert, why don't you write a chapter on love?"

"I don't need to write about love! I *exude* love." Broody stalked away from the desk and peered out the window. "I could make anyone in this whole village of characters fall in love with me."

"Oh?" Blondie said, looking out the window, too. Right now, they were in some sort of a historical setting. The dystopian setting of earlier in the day must have just been a passing fad. New Story City changed often. Women with parasols paraded past, while carriages carrying more supporting characters rattled down the cobblestone streets. It wasn't clear exactly what century they were in but, then again, it never was.

Luckily, the corset Blondie wore was specifically designed for an actual antagonist with nefarious plots she had to accomplish, so it would never cause her to faint in a moment of great excitement. "I'm sure you could," she finally admitted. After all, even her character arc, as wicked as it was, still involved loving him. "You know who we should talk to? As research for your chapter on love?"

"I've already had a long talk with my reflection," Broody assured her. "He gives such good advice."

She put a hand to her temple, wondering exactly what anyone—herself, the other love interests, and heck, even the Author—could ever see in Broody.

And then he smiled at her with that dazzling, blinding, brilliant smile, and her knees went weak.

Just a little.

"C'mon, hot stuff." She grabbed his arm and dragged him away from his desk. Didn't he know only Authors could get away with sitting and staring at an unfinished book for hours on end?

Outside, the day was lovely, and everyone they passed seemed to be in an absolutely wonderful mood. "Cheerio, my good fellows!" Broody called, and then turned to Blondie. "We appear to be in Londonish-land today."

"Again. Lovely," she replied drily. Why was it *always* London. She turned, searching the street for the person she'd wanted Broody to speak with. In a historical novel, a Broody would never live next door to the heroine. She was probably away at a finishing school, anyway.

He'd be working somewhere . . . like a blacksmith shop! Perfect.

They crossed the street to find a young man with sandy blond hair, a more wholesome shade than Blondie's own, hammering a sword. Despite the anvil and other tools usually found in a blacksmith's shop, the work didn't seem to be going well. His motions were rather imprecise, as it was clear his Author had never researched exactly how to make a sword.

Also, his shirt was open enough to reveal powerful muscles, and also to run the risk of third-degree burns.

Not like that ever happened. Shirtless guys were practically impervious to all elements in fiction.

But from the wholesome hair to the good-natured humming, this character exuded niceness. In other words, it was the person she had sought.

Broody's rival. The boy next door. The Nice Guy.

"Good day," he said, giving up on the project. "How can I help . . . Oh, it's you." He folded his arms and glared. "Sir Broodington."

"Uh. Just Broody is fine." He rubbed the back of his head, clearly uncomfortable with this turn of events. "Blondie," he whispered harshly, "I thought you were taking me to someone who could help me write about love."

"I did." She smirked. "Who knows more about love than the other guy in your love triangle?"

The two men sputtered, shocked at the notion that they'd actually have to work together.

"Now, you two stop groaning, and start talking."

"But . . . but he's a jerk!" the rival cried.

"And he's a girlfriend-stealing, manners-having, parents-charming meanie-head!" Broody responded.

Blondie gritted her teeth. If she were a true pro-tagonist, the new girl, or the Chosen One, these ridiculous men would be overjoyed to help her.

Instead, she was a villain, and they were annoyed.

"Look," she said, crossing her arms. "Between the two of you, you've won the hearts of practically every protagonist ever. I'm sure a quick chat will unravel all the mysteries of love."

The two heroes exchanged gemstone-colored glares, sapphire flashing against brilliant emerald. Blondie tapped her foot. The staring continued. She checked her anachronistic watch. They were still staring.

Finally, the today-a-blacksmith boy whose name she couldn't even remember—she always thought of him as Nice Guy—grudgingly said, "Broody, it's always an honor to be in love triangles with you."

"Uh. Same to you . . . pal."

So Broody didn't know the guy's name either. Poor fellow.

Nice Guy sighed. "It does get exhausting, you know. All that bickering, and trying to outdo your grand romantic gestures and . . ."

"And all those brawls the Authors make us have," Broody said. "Exhausting. And then the girl, she never appreciates any of our efforts! She just sits there, smiling mildly at us while all the readers divide into #TeamYou and #TeamMe."

"I think I'm #TeamNeedsANap," Nice Guy said.

Broody . . . actually laughed. He patted him on the back in a stereotypically masculine way.

Blondie edged away, aware she was intruding on a moment of much needed character development.

When she returned a few hours later, after finding a protagonist and subtly insulting her gown, which always improved her mood, Blondie found the two guys still chatting.

"Ah, good, you're back." Broody sprang to his feet and waved goodbye to his . . . rival.

"Let's get that drink soon. Soda for you, stolen whiskey for me, am I right?" Broody even winked at him.

For the love of all things pink, glittery, and dangerous, what had she done?

"So, uh, Broody," she began, still baffled by this turn of events. Darn it. She was dealing with main characters. Of course plot twists would occur more frequently. "You get some good advice for your book?"

He shrugged. "Maybe. But I'm still the expert."

"Of course you are," she replied, her tone drier than the driest thing in the world, which was very dry.

"But it's interesting. Did you know . . . he's . . . sometimes he thinks he's in love with someone ELSE?" Broody was practically shouting. Luckily, all of the nearby supporting characters were used to his drama, so they ignored him.

"Ah, how strange." Broody must have found it shocking to realize that the world didn't revolve around him and his love interest. That there could be characters who would pine for and kiss and hope for the love of characters who were not him. Who might never even come close to being main characters.

"But aren't you surprised?" he asked, genuinely confused.

"No."

Blondie shook her head. It wasn't at all surprising that another character would want more than the life they were trapped in. After all, wasn't that what she wanted, too?

But soon Broody would write all the secrets she'd need, and then she'd finally, *finally* be able to become a main character herself.

CHAPTER 4

FINDING TRUE LOVE

Not every story has a love story, and that's totally fine! But, since I've starred in a lot of love stories, I thought I'd share my notes.

While there are various types of plots, there are also various types of love stories.

Young adult literature gets made fun of a lot by so-called grown-ups for always having love stories (even though it doesn't) and for over-using "ridiculous love triangles" (even though there are plenty of stories without one) and for "always being about vampires and silly girls." (Seriously, it's like these "adults" read one YA book ten years ago and based all their opinions on that.)

To these critics, I say, I'm sorry you're so incredibly bitter and miserable that you can't feel that rush of joy when your crush smiles at imagine what butterflies in your stomach feel like. Also, please read some YA before insulting it.

If you want to be in a YA story without a love story, I know you will be absolutely amazing at it! Feel free to skip this chapter.

And if you don't want your love story to have kisses, that's fine, too. I guess?

Yes, Broody. It is more than fine to have a story without kissing and/or without a love story. Everyone should be a protagonist, not just people with love stories. I don't expect you to understand this, because you're a clueless oaf. Dearest reader: focus on telling your own story. It's going to be incredible, no matter what.

xoxo, B

For all of you awesome people who love, love, love LOVE, and all of its mushy, magical magnificence, come closer. Peer into my gemstone-colored eyes. Swoon into my strong, protective arms.

What, exactly, is love?

This is a difficult question, to be sure, but one I absolutely, positively know the answer to. Obviously I know it, even though it seems every poet, artist, and overzealous karaoke singer is constantly searching to define just what is the essence of this great mystery so many seek. Mainly because I know everything.

And because I am an expert at everything.

And I'm always in love.

So. What is love? It is . . . the sound of two heartbeats synchronizing perfectly. The universe sparkling in someone else's eyes. Your own face on a giant billboard advertising your movie.

Basically, love should give you a great sense of peace and happiness. Or the warm fuzzies.

Or at least a three-book deal.

Now, let's cover the most important part of any proper main character's life:

Finding True Love

Ready? No, of course you're not. True love should surprise you, like a girl colliding with you in a high school hallway or a mysterious (possibly nonhuman) handsome man saving you from a supernatural threat.

Now, some people will tell you love isn't everything, but guess what? They're wrong! As Shakespeare himself said, "Love is . . ." Well, okay. I can't remember the quote. There weren't any main characters in my English lit class, so I skipped it . . . for the past thirty years. The point is, love is superduper important. And you should totally look up that Shakespeare quote and put it in italics on the first page of your novel so people know it's a totally deep and very romantic book.

Love is waaaaaay better than friendship. I mean, who needs friends, right? All they do is support you and give you advice and remind you when you're being a jerk. *Pfffft.* What a waste of time.

At the very least, it's important to meet the love of your life before page 50. Let's make like a transfer student and jump right into the drama, shall we?

Traits of a Great Love Interest

Quick note: I know I had some great words about love interests being any gender, but since I'm giving you advice based on my own love life (love lives?) I'm just going to use "her" as that's 99 percent of my relationships. And I'm only saying that because historically, that's what happened. These days, I've gotten to star in relationships with many amazing characters of all pronouns.

What separates any average character from a love interest? Easy.

Ordinariness.

I mean it. The perfect love interest should be so, so, *so* ordinary that reality warps around her, causing plot to happen. She should remind her reflection of her ordinariness at least once per day, and three times in a first chapter.

Ideal ordinary traits include: frizzy hair, an eye color that is "plain," shortness, a body type that she'll refer to as "fat" despite being much smaller than the average American teen, and a nose she doesn't like.

Oh, and she'll be white.

Other traits that make a good love interest? Disinterest in anything aside from me, a lack of personal ambition aside from marrying me, and being part of a prophecy or curse (also involving me). In general, her life should be structured so that she spends every hour, every minute, waiting for me to show up.

A good love interest has very few friends . . . or none at all. And why should she? She's not like other girls. And friends might caution her against trusting me, which is stupid. I'm totally trustworthy . . . except for the billions of lies I've told her. But those are just . . . misunderstandings, right?

On a similar note, any time I meet an orphan, I fall in love with her faster than you can preorder my next book online. Orphans are *always* main characters, and usually hidden princesses, too. Plus, they have no family to point out what a terrible boyfriend you are.

In general, you should have very little knowledge about your love interest before you two make smoldering eye contact. Everyone knows that being friends first never ends in true love. Friendship is for your rival in the love triangle; he's a loser.

Ideally, she'll be new to the school/kingdom/space station. Or, at the very least, new to you—summer makeovers always make a character *so much* more appealing. Just be sure you reassure her that you love her heart, not her looks. (Although you'd dump her in a second if she stopped looking all pretty and made-over. But she doesn't need to know that.)

Or, if she's not new to your setting, be new to hers. You know. Show up in town with your motorcycle, a vow to never talk about your past, and some drama. Works every time. Love interests never wait longer than five minutes after meeting me before declaring their love. (Unlike any self-respecting Broody. Insta-declarations of love come from the Nice Guy Next Door or a nerdy male best friend . . . Those guys aren't worth your time. Why would you want a supportive, considerate love interest who could have . . . me?)

Ways to Meet the Love of Your Life

Speaking of motorcycles, here are some surefire ways to meet your one true love. Number one: Run for your life. It doesn't matter if you're fleeing from an alien invasion, a tornado, or an angry ex-girlfriend. (Yours, not hers. She's never dated anyone before you. Obviously.) Fleeing is always a great way to hold hands, make good eye contact, and fall deeply in love.

Close encounters of the romantic kind are often called "meet-cutes." They're a bright spot in any story, and I've got several more ways to help you cutely run into the love of your life:

As these are all my favorite types, let's assume you're an aspiring Broody as you read these.

• **Get involved in some sort of dystopian plot.** These things are really good at pairing off (heterosexual) ridiculously attractive teenagers, and always leads them to fall in love as they fight the evil, evil government in a nation that is most definitely not on a future version of Earth.

• **Be bad at a school subject.** Girls *love* teaching. They love teaching almost as much as they love babies. Therefore, if you show absolutely no skill in an academic subject, she'll be able to help you pass that test so you can play in the big game.

Caveat: All girls are bad at math and science. When it comes to those subjects, they will be looking for a handsome male to instruct them, as STEM topics are too hard for pretty-little-main-female-protagonist brains.

Oh, and they should also be terrible at walking. A good love interest trips at least five times a day.

• **Be born into a family currently feuding with another family.** Over anything. A blood feud is just as good as any die-hard sports rivalry to create star-crossed lovers.

• **If you're a supernatural creature, try to find a girl who has no idea of her destiny and obsessively follow her around.** Girls *love* that. The creepier you are, the better.

• **Cause a dangerous situation.** Chase that fearsome monster you've been tracking right into the coffee shop where an innocent young main character is studying. After the monster smashes the table and spills her latte, you'll slay the beast, and she'll be so grateful to you that she'll neglect to point out you were the one who endangered her life in the first place.

• **Throw a party at her house.** You know how you have a crush on the most sheltered, least likely to party girl in the whole school? Well, her parents are going to be out of town this Friday, so you should definitely throw a party at her house to impress her.

• **Declare you'll never fall in love.** You know what Authors love doing to main characters? Making us regret whatever we declare loudly and dramatically. Therefore, if you ever want something to happen in your story, all you have to do is very loudly state that it will never happen, and *ta-da*!

How Can You Create Love?

Simple. Be loving, kind, considerate, and patient. Learn everything about your love interest you can, be there for them whenever they need you, and always put them first. Take time to let the relationship grow like a delicate, priceless flower that needs attention and tender care.

Or . . . skip all that and use one of these handy insta-romance spritzes. No main character has

actual time to manage a relationship from scratch. Plus, if you're
too kind, you're going to hurt
your love triangle score (more about
that on page 180). Considerate is the
opposite of swoony.

To save you time, I've highlighted
some highly powerful scents
that you can spritz on to help
develop your main character
style. They're guaranteed to
win you love, cement your main
character status, and maybe even
get you kissed. Just like you can use
Febreze when you don't feel like
cleaning your house, the below scents are
guaranteed to tidy up any love story:

Star-Crossed Lovers Spritz

Scent: The beautiful but doomed combination of a
rose left out in the cold, unfeeling snow, and a single teardrop glistening on a vibrant red petal.

When to Use: If you and your beloved are from opposing sides of anything. One of you is made of ice, and
the other is made of fire. Your family is descended
from a long line of tea aficionados, and hers, coffee
junkies. You're a die-hard Yankees, fan and she'll

never stop cheering for the Red Sox. Whatever the reason, the plot is determined to rip you two asunder.

Warning: Uh, yeah. You'll probably be ripped asunder. But at least you'll smell really good first!

The Bodyguard Musk

Scent: The protective aroma of a strong oak tree embracing you, even though it ought to just stand all strong and treelike in the woodsy forest. Alone.

When to Use: Let's say you've been ordered to protect a beautiful person. Conveniently enough, you also happen to be attracted to said beautiful person. Your boss also orders you to not kiss the human who is, of course, the most stunning, lovely, funniest person you've ever met in your entire life. (But mainly, they're really just beautiful. Who cares about that personality stuff, right?) This spray will ensure that you two will fall madly in love . . . despite your status as their bodyguard. Really, why doesn't your boss assign you to protect people who are entirely repellant? Wouldn't that be easier?

Warning: You're probably protecting the love interest from something deadly. This scent may cloud your warrior senses, resulting in you becoming injured in the line of duty.

Culture Clash Body Spray

Scent: The odd but pleasant combination of flowers and vegetables. With the crispness of carrot and the lushness of peony, united to form a pleasant mist. Not to be confused with the far more intense scent of star-crossed lovers.

When to Use: You don't necessarily hate each other, but you certainly have nothing in common. One of you loves Pepsi, puppies, and peppermint toothpaste while the other lives for Coke, cats, and cotton candy.

Authors love nothing more than running a joke into the ground.

Warning: As this scent lasts a short time, it may be hard to maintain a lasting relationship with someone you have nothing in common with. Let's cross our fingers it gets you through the entire book.

Eau de Fake Relationship

Scent: The strangely sweet scent of a perfume sprayed onto fake flowers, with just a hint of the about-to-bloom real deal.

When to Use: Let's face it. Sometimes you need to have a fake relationship . . . for reasons. Perhaps you're a secret agent and need a good cover. Or you're hiding from your world-destroying evil ex. Maybe you have an insanely wealthy eccentric aunt who's promised to make you her sole heir on the condition that you're in a relationship. Gotta love those eccentric aunts who make plot happen.

Regardless of the reason, you've got to create the illusion of dating someone, or you'll end up in big trouble. No, I have no idea why the plot states that you'll end up broke/dead/a social pariah if you're not dating someone. Just blame the patriarchy, okay? So, rather than that awkward situation of asking out someone you really like and with whom you could have a meaningful connection, dab a little of this cologne on and imbue yourself with fake relationship magic.

Warning: Well, your fake significant other is going to fall in love with you, 100 percent guaranteed. Hopefully that doesn't cause any problems in your already incredibly complicated life.

Spoiler alert: It will. Or there wouldn't be a book.

Stranger-Dangerously-In-Love Spray

Scent: The intense, full bloom of a high-speed car chase followed by some improbably large explosions, coupled with the refreshing lemony fragrance of witty banter.

When to Use: You're facing a really, *really* big problem: the world is ending. Or prom is canceled. There's no way you can save the day on your own. No matter how great a main character you are, some things are impossible to achieve alone.

Like the tango.

Or flying a spaceship.

Same skill set, really.

This scent will draw to you a perfect companion who will help save the day. You've simply never met them before.

Warning: With that intense gunpowder smell of explosions, you may never get more than one kiss. It's well known that in action movies, a main character's aroma of attraction brings them a different love interest in each sequel. And, just like being a bodyguard, there's a lot of danger associated, so a love interest might . . . er . . . die.

Loathing to Love Lotion

Scent: The overpowering stench of overripe fruit that blossoms into the sweet, rarest jasmine.

When to Use: You can't stand someone. At *all*. It's not even that they're your opposite (although, we've got a scent for that, too). Every little thing he does makes you want to rip his hair out.

Until one day you grab a strand to do just that and immediately notice how incredibly silky and soft and beautifully scented it is. Everything changes in that moment, as his beautiful curls wrap around your fingers like silky ribbons. You cannot hate him anymore, despite absolutely none of his personality changing. You are in love.

Warning: The constant bickering caused by early application of this scent can be very annoying to friends, family members, and even the birds in the trees above you.

Rivalry, the new Fragrance from Bestselling Author

Scent: The warring aromas of coffee and hot chocolate, twining sensuously in a dance of competitive and romantic bliss.

When to Use: You have a goal: Get the highest grade on the test, or take over the world, or be the best ice-skater in town, and someone else—someone gorgeously, stupidly, obnoxiously talented, with far more privilege than you—also wants the same thing. Usually it's a stupid boy, giving him all the powers of the patriarchy you might expect, including far more wealth and social status than you yourself have.

That's okay! You're spunky! You'll sew your own outfit, use cute rhymes on flash cards, and assemble a lovable, supportive group of other slightly quirky misfits to stand up against your powerful, rich rival.

Great! . . . Except your rival is really, *really* cute.

Perhaps . . . perhaps you two can work together after all?

Warning: This sweet, richly aromatic scent may suddenly vanish, allowing you to realize your rival only seduced you to win the competition.

Bet No. 5

Scent: The thrilling, novel concept of placing a bet on a romantic moment of your life, chased directly by the strong, confusing crushed-petal scent of regret.

When to Use: You are absolutely certain that you will be able to avoid the time-wasting idiocy of love, and have vocally made this known to all around you. Clearly, you should couple that boast with direct action, so spritz on this scent, thus ensuring that you will, in fact, fall madly in love.

Warning: Alas, there must always be someone on the other side of the bet—the sniffer of this beautiful perfume. Are you so sure you want to turn a sweet, young love interest's affections into a game?

Oh, you are?

Well, carry on, then.

Eau de Mutually Being in Love . . . Secretly

Scent: The fragile, soft aroma of sweet almost-kisses, buttercups, and words left unsaid.

When to Use: You and your love interest are in love with one another but can't admit it. Once you apply this perfume, each of you will realize you love the other one. But, hold on! Don't ring the wedding bells/prepare the prom dress/summon the masquerade ball planners just yet. Due to the nature of this confusing, never-the-perfect-moment scent, you will declare your new found realization to literally everyone in the story except the person you're madly in love with. You may *never* be able to actually confess your true feelings to your intended . . . At least not until the very end of the story.

Warning: This scent usually attracts more than one love interest. And what better way to ensure that you will never confess your undying ardor to your one true love than becoming entangled in a relationship with someone completely different?

Friendship Blossoms to Love Blast

Scent: The bright, overly chipper fragrance of brownies and flower buds, frosted with aggravatingly annoying, Broody-free potential.

When to use: Wait. Your friend is your love interest? Who would ever want to fall in love with their friend when there's a sexy, broody, ridiculously good-looking and also potentially dangerous stranger in their life?

I mean, seriously. He's some nice, respectful guy you've known forever and I'm, well, a hot, rude stranger.

This is an *easy choice*. (Just so we're clear, the choice is me.) Sometimes characters get confused and make the wrong decision. Like when they try to apply this scent, not realizing how much better I am.

Reader, Broody is just sad because he's never had any friends fall in love with him. Ignore all this.

xoxo, B

Warning: Using this scent will blind you to how incredibly attractive that broody, dark, and mysterious other guy is. You'll probably miss out on the love of a lifetime.

###

So, there's your basic rundown of romantic relationships, or *ships* as the cool kids call them these days. Believe me, I'm captain of an entire armada of ships.

Now we've arrived at the biggest of all relationship-related things, the veritable mother*ship* of all ships: LOVE TRIANGLES.

What's a love triangle?

I tend to skip all my classes except for chemistry—my love interest will always be my lab partner—but you wanna know what class I never missed?

Geometry. I wanted to be 100 percent positive I understood how a triangle worked, so I could always win any one I found myself stuck in.

In geometry, I learned a formula that is sure to help if you find yourself in a love triangle:

$$a^2 + b^2 = c^2$$

Some Greek guy invented it, probably because he, too, was frustrated when he couldn't beat his rival for someone's heart. Bet he spent hours brooding in his toga, debating how best to win the affections of the pretty girl with the pet Pegasus who lived up the road. Then, *bam*, because he's a secret genius—all of us Broodys are—he finally figured out the formula:

a = all the swoony things you do
b = beauty/broodiosity/best used adjectives
c = chance of winning the love triangle

I'm not sure why those tiny twos are there. Maybe they're decorations, like pretty prom corsages.

So, basically, if you're not a particularly good-looking main character, or your Author was a bit skimpy on describing the particular gemstone-like qualities of your eyes, don't worry. You can still win this love triangle! You just have to do extra swoonworthy things.

Let's look at *Beauty and the Beast*. That dude is *so* not swoonworthy. But he gives Belle a library! We all know that every single female love interest adores reading, so he gets maximum swoon points there.

What if you happen to be almost as incredibly good-looking as I am? Well, good news, you'll have to do almost no work to ensure your eventual triumph in the triangle.

As always, it is a good idea to review my notes on your rivals, and be sure to never let your guard down. I know a few main characters who lost out on a love triangle with only fifty pages of the third book left.

A NOTE FROM SOMEONE WHO ISN'T IN LOVE

Hey. Blondie, here. Again. With another little interruption for content Broody has forgotten to mention.

I'll be honest with you. (Shocking, I know. It's a new thing for me.) I've never won a love triangle in my life. Even my much nicer cousin, Pathetica DePressa, who always gets stuck being that "female friend with an ill-fated crush" has never won a love triangle. At least she played an incredibly popular role in some French musical about barricades.

But because I've never gotten to have a happily ever after, I've learned a thing or two.

Mainly, that life can still be awesome without love. And love isn't even always romantic, or based on stupid perfume scents. Characters who don't have love, or who don't want love, or who have the love of their friends, are just as deserving of the spotlight. Don't listen to Broody. He acts like the only stories that matter are the ones with batting eyelashes and fluttering hearts.

Me? All I want is my own story. My own role. I don't care if there's love in it or not.

xoxo, B

CHAPTER 5

EVEN MORE ABOUT LOVE

Right. So I've shared all my favorite scents, and all about my favorite shapes of love. What more could you want to know? Haven't you gone out there and started kissing people yet?

Ohhh. I've forgotten to tell you how to do that! Right. Let's dive right in.

oh, goodie.
    xoxo, B

How to Get a First Kiss

Let me set the scene.

You've found a love interest. You've bantered and blushed, batted eyelashes and battled evil together. And now, the setting around you becomes more vivid, more magical. Sudden stars appear in the sky, shining almost as bright as your own gemstone eyes. Flowers never before mentioned bloom and carry their scent on the sweet breeze. Your heart beats harder in your chest. You're relieved to find out your heart is still *in* your chest and not in your feet.

But all these details spell out one thing:

Your first kiss is about to happen.

One of the absolute best parts of true love is that illustrious, wonderful moment known as THE FIRST KISS. Granted, I, as a broody, attractive male, have never been concerned with my first kiss, only my last first kiss (unless I get brainwashed, forget you, and kiss someone else). But most female main characters should spend at least the first three chapters agonizing over this incredibly important moment.

Well, worry no more! I've assembled some great ways get your first kiss:

The Big Dance

Ah. A classic. There's a dance (preferably with a seasonally appropriate theme) and you've found a dress, lost the plot, and are ready for a kiss.

Fight

This is like dancing, except with weapons. As you're swinging large, sharp, dangerous metal things at one another, sneak in a kiss, too. Don't worry. Accidental beheadings never occur.

Run Somewhere Together

All couples are capable of running in perfect synchronization while holding hands, which means they can also kiss without tripping while they're running.

Get Stuck Somewhere

I'm just saying, if you get trapped in a room together, you're probably going to end up kissing.

Sleep Somewhere

No matter where you travel, there will always only be one bed. Therefore, the following will happen. One person will offer to sleep on the floor. The other will insist they can share the bed. There will be cuddling, and then kissing.

Huddle Together for Warmth

Shivering always leads to kissing. Because kissing prevents hypothermia.

Sing Together

I don't know, my friend. The end of a romantic duet is always a kiss.

Touch Her Face

For any reason. Maybe you need to brush hair out of her eyes. Maybe you want to wipe a tear away. Maybe she has spinach stuck in her teeth. Any reason at all to touch her face is a good reason. After all, we all know love interests don't care about personal space.

Really, take advantage of any task you can do together, as long as there are moments for long, lingering eye contact.

True Love

What, exactly, is true love? Is it different than normal love? Absolutely. It is as unlike average, boring, basic love as the color "star-struck sapphire" is from "blue."

True love is when you realize that you want to spend the rest of your life (or at least the next 103 pages) with another character. It's usually something that should be declared ... if not by defiantly shouting to the heavens, then at least whispered into your true love's ear.

At the very least, true love is what sells all our books and movies we star in, am I right?

Why is love so important?

Uh, because it's the most powerful force in the galaxy, duh. There are very few things love can't do. It's especially good for expanding page counts, providing you armies of fans, and enabling you to accrue lots and lots of adjectives.

It's also, you know, just plain fun.

What else can it do? Pretty much anything. I've seen characters come back from death if their true love kisses them. I've seen a declaration of true love enable a guy to find his love interest who disappeared in the middle of New York. All the guy had to do was shout, "I love her!" and traffic vanished and a cab appeared. I've even seen true love help two characters land scholarships to both attend the exact same college.

I mean, love can even break the laws of science. I hear you scoffing. *Okay, Broody, so maybe the others are possible, but this one seems downright ridiculous.*

You're wrong. If the evil villain has placed a curse on your beloved, rendering her unable to breathe, the love of your life should probably die in, like ... thirty seconds. Two minutes, max.

But if you declare your true, undying, eternal, perfect love for her while you battle the evil dude?

Trust me, that girl will be able to hold her breath forever.

That, my friends, is the power of true love overcoming the laws of science.

True love is beautiful and wonderful and a clear marker of main character status, although I'm told some protagonists go through an entire book series never finding it. How sad.

I can assure you that's never happened to me. I've never had a problem securing my one-true-love status with my love interests. And if there were possibly books in which I didn't win the heart of my one true love? Well . . . we don't need to talk about those.

ARE YOU IN LOVE?

Have you noticed something different about your breathing or your heartbeat?

1. Yes.
2. No.
3. Um, no? But your breath stinks.

Have you gotten called out for daydreaming in class?

1. Huh? Oh, yeah. Sorry, I was just daydreaming now.
2. No.
3. Nope. I have gotten detention for plotting to ruin prom, though.

How many friends do you currently have?

1. None. They just didn't understand me, you know? Always saying how I never have time for them anymore, and I'm too busy daydreaming/staring at a certain someone . . .
2. A perfectly respectable amount for a fictional character (so, no more than three).
3. I don't have friends. I have minions.

What color are the eyes you're daydreaming about?

1. The most cerulean-sapphire shade of blue, with hints of deep ocean blue and flecks of gold.
2. Brown.
3. I'm not daydreaming about anything besides vengeance.

Have you blushed/stuttered/felt like you might faint recently?

1. YES! All the time.
2. Nope.
3. No way. And if you feel like that, you might have food poisoning.

What did the antagonist last say to you?

1. "Aw, what a cute couple! It would be a shame if anything happened to one of you."
2. "Who are you again?"
3. "Oh, hey, nice seeing you. Let's catch up soon. Coffee date?"

Mostly 1s:
Yup. It's love. I predict your first kiss is coming within fifty pages.

Mostly 2s:
Sad to say, you're not in love yet. Give it time.

Mostly 3s:
Fess up. You're really Blondie DeMeani, aren't you?

So You've Landed a Love Interest. What Do You Do with 'em?

Be careful! The last thing you want is to be the losing person in a love triangle because you failed to maintain the affection of your love interest. This leads me to the number one thing you must do once you've acquired a love interest: become unpredictable.

You know what girls hate? When you tell the truth, show up on time, and communicate effectively.

Always make sure you have at least one lie and a couple of secrets you refuse to tell her about. The more times you answer her questions with only stormy silence, the harder she'll fall in love.

Here is an example of two truths and a lie, created by yours truly. Can you figure out which is the lie?

1. My favorite breakfast food is pancakes arranged in the shape of a snowman, with chocolate chip buttons and candy canes for arms.

2. My ideal date is the circus.

3. My kisses are so incredible, they have actually stopped my love interests' hearts before.

If you guessed that number two is the lie, you're right. I can't stand clowns. Those guys scare me more than a cliffhanger ending.

But while you want to maintain a mysterious aloofness, if you ignore a love interest *too* well, she'll run off with your rival, or your best friend, or your brother. I recommend that you break down your time as follows: ignore her 60 percent of the time, lie 30 percent, evade 9 percent, and be romantic with that last 1 percent.

If you're ever unsure how long you've spent doing each of these tasks, you might try answering your love interest's questions with a cryptic smile and/or a mysterious statement.

Mysterious and yet romantic things to say include:

1. I've never known anyone like you before.
2. It's too soon.
3. It's too late.
4. All of this is happening too fast.
5. There are so many things I can't tell you.
6. The clowns are coming. Run!

7. Will you be patient with me?
8. Don't forget me.
9. Please, forget me.
10. Seriously, in case you forgot, clowns are creepy.
11. I think I'm falling for you.
12. I turn into a hedgehog when the moon is full.
13. There's something I need to tell you.

Perhaps none of those romantic lines feel quite right to you in the moment, and you've found yourself facing a terrible, daunting, inevitable task: you've got to take your love interest out on a date.

Scary, right?

It's one thing to topple dystopian regimes together. But planning a date? That seems so much harder.

Don't panic.

Romantic dates abound for a main character and a love interest. Really, as long as you are a couple, anything you do can be romantic! I've had amazing dates just staring into my love interests' eyes. Slaying zombies is good, too. The sky's the limit. Unless she wants to go on a double date. *Always* avoid those. Your ideal love interest should have no other friends, so this will not be a problem.

Sure, you may now smell good enough to attract true love, but keeping your love interest is not going to be a walk in the park. Well, except for when you two are literally walking in the park. But be prepared: you'll probably get attacked by clowns or something.

As a main character in love, you have a target painted on your back. Everyone, from the smallest monster-of-the-week to the biggest, baddest evil baddie, suddenly has no greater goal than to destroy your true love. The moment your antagonist even catches a whiff of the scent of love, they will hunt you down with the sole aim of stealing away your true love from you.

Sometimes it seems like the bad guys are more focused on my love life than actually taking over the world. Weird, right?

Trouble in Paradise— Surviving a Breakup

I've got bad news for you. No matter how pure your love is or how much excellent eye contact you two have exchanged, you and the object of your affection are probably going to break up.

At least for a chapter.

Wanna know why?

Readers.

Those annoying humans *hate* when a couple just gets together and stays together forever.

As a result, your Author is going to make trouble for you and your love interest. This may include, but is not limited to:

- **Releasing the evil exes (yours):** We've certainly covered these in our exploration of antagonist roles, but as a reminder, if you're dating someone at the start of the novel, they will absolutely turn out to be evil after you dump them.

- **Interruptions from strict parents (hers):** Rather than getting her parents to understand and like you, just practice climbing into her bedroom. Your love interest's room will always be located on the second floor, and the climb will always be completely doable.

- **Interference from evil parents (yours):** I'm not sure why your father, the mayor/overlord/head-vampire has decided that it is more important to meddle in your love life than carrying out any of the tasks related to his day job, but that's the way it is.

- **Being kidnapped (either of you, really):** Probably one of the above meddlers carried out said kidnapping.

- **Finding out you're engaged to someone else (usually you):** A betrothed you don't know about functions in the exact same manner as an evil ex, coupled with the additional annoying binding authority of the law.

- **Being brainwashed:** It happens. A lot. Oddly enough, your love interest will never believe it could happen to you.

• **A ginormous misunderstanding that you two simply refuse to talk through:** Communication is stupid.

Don't worry. You'll usually manage to get through whatever terrible forces have torn you and your love interest apart. If you don't, there's always the sequel!

Can you navigate the complicated and dangerous Maze of Love without getting your heart broken?

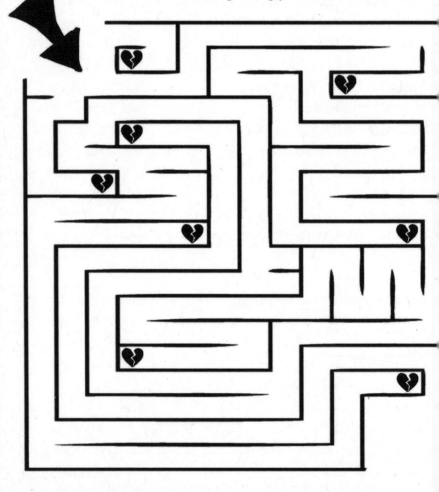

But Broody, you ask, *how do I get my love interest back?*

Well, do something really, really romantic. Save her life or buy her a prom dress (remember how I told you to take all of her measurements while you were watching her sleep?) or skip your big game to attend her birthday party. (You already secured the state championship, so it doesn't really matter.) Maybe try overthrowing a government to impress her.

Try apologizing to her dad for your general terrible-boyfriend behavior. It's a well-known fact that men control the romantic lives of all women, so this gesture will so impress your love interest, she'll never leave your side again.

Also, I've been using "her" because these are all actual times I've won a girl back. I could totally get an ex-boyfriend to love me again using these same techniques, I'm sure. Substitute pronouns in examples above as needed.

Another option: don't apologize at all. Remind her of your tragic backstory/your evil father/how difficult your life is as a ridiculously attractive, wealthy main character. She'll feel bad for you and immediately forgive all the terrible things you've done.

You've found a love interest, got them to fall madly in love with you, went on a few romantic dates, ignored them a ton, and survived the threatened breakup.

Excellent.

Now what?

Well, you have to ensure that, despite knowing one another for less than the amount of time it takes to order a pizza, what you two have is absolutely 100 percent true, never-ending love.

No pressure.

How do you do that? Sleep together? *False!* Sleeping together is very dangerous and can get your book banned or cause something tragic to happen in-story. You wouldn't believe how many babies are born after one night of passion and then the father wanders into some war/curse/dystopia and DIES.

Why would you risk this?

If you have to, just roll around in a bunch of metaphors. You know, flowery stuff. Heck, you might even try rolling around in some actual flowers.

But there are other options to ensure your epic romance never wavers that are far less dangerous:

- **Bring her into your supernatural creature club.** If you're a werelemur, bite her so she can be one, too. If you're an elf, find some sort of magical reason for her to be by your side forever. If you're a vampire . . . *psssh*, why am I giving vampires advice? You all have that "true love lasts forever" stuff down.

- **If you're in a band, make her your lead singer.** Yes, even if the only singing she ever did was into a hairbrush in her own room. She's a main character. She'll have no problem suddenly becoming a rock star.

- **Remind her that her destiny revolves around you and, therefore, all her future goals should, as well.** It is a fact: your dreams are always more important than hers.

- **Get married.** Granted, this is much easier in a fantasy world or in historical fiction, but wait until the sequel or the sequel's sequel, and it might just happen.

- **Adopt something together.** A park. A puppy. A scrappy orphan who needs a loving home.

- **Attend the same college.** Don't worry, somehow both of you will get scholarships to the exact same school, which will also have the perfect major for both of you.

- OPTIONAL AND VERY RISKY BUT ALSO VERY SEXY MOVE: **Don't secure true love status.** Leave town with a promise to fix yourself and come back someday when you've become a better man for her. Fans will love you forever and write you tons more fan fiction (for more on that subject, see page 313) than all these other approaches combined.

Okay, so by now you might be thinking that love is a lot of work. I'm going to tell you that's . . . er . . . true. Sort of.

I mean, look, love *is* work, yes, but it's not like you have to keep it up for more than two years. You are a YA character, so as long as you have a true love by the time you're eighteen, you'll always have one, at least in the reader's mind. Maybe all YA characters part ways at age twenty. I wouldn't know. I've never been older than seventeen. (Or, like, 17,000 years old, but I still look sixteen. And act like a six-year-old.)

So just hang in there. Find a good smell, spritz yourself. Make sure your hair is perfectly tousled. Let it shade your gemstone-colored eyes. Practice your lopsided smile. (But make sure your smile reaches your eyes! You're a main character, not an antagonist.)

Lovely.

Now go out there and make some romance happen.

NARRATIVE INTERLUDE: WHILE OUR HEROIC HERO COWERS, EVIL LAUGHS

Blondie leaned on the doorframe of Broody's room, watching him write. Surrounded by his various medals and trophies, all of which reflected the golden highlights subtly shining in his dark mane, Broody seemed completely engrossed in what he was writing. She'd never seen him so focused on anything—aside from staring into reflective surfaces.

Watching someone else write turned out to be fascinating. She'd never been friends with bookish or writerly types. After all, they were her sworn enemies. And she'd never felt much fondness for the Authors themselves. If they were too lazy to give her a good character arc, why bother? Male villains were given amazing arcs all the time. Sometimes, they even had larger fan bases than the heroines. But as far as evil female characters were concerned . . .

They got nothing.

Heck, sometimes the Authors even wrote Blondie as illiterate or as a book-hater because they were trying to make her feel even more isolated from the world of writers and characters.

Broody sneezed.

"Bless you."

He jumped at the sound of her voice, then turned and blinked at her like a very confused puppy, who'd just been caught rolling in something he shouldn't have. The surprise only lasted a moment before he leaned one arm on the back of his plush chair, which was as over-padded as his ego. "Oh, it's you."

"Surprise." She rolled her eyes. "I'm bored. My latest Author kicked me out of the narrative in the fourth chapter."

He muttered something she wasn't sure she quite caught, but it sounded a lot like, "At least you got to be in chapters."

Well-versed in catching what other characters muttered, Blondie narrowed her eyes. Was

Broody . . . Was there another reason he was working on this project? Time passed strangely for fictional characters, certainly, but it did seem like Broody suddenly had an awful lot of free time.

Almost as much free time as the pack of vampires she knew, who hadn't gotten to be in a book in years.

Could Broody be on hiatus?

No. Surely not. He couldn't be. Authors adored him. "How's the book?" she asked.

"It's awesome. All the supporting characters in all the fictional worlds are gonna love me!" He paused, winked rakishly at her (a different wink from his seductive one, and completely unrelated to the one he used when he was joking), and added, "Even more than they already do."

Tilting her head so her perfect blonde curls slid perfectly over a shoulder, she asked, her tone even more perfectly styled than her hair or her head tilt, "Broody . . . how many characters do you know?"

"Lots," he muttered, chewing on the end of his pencil and trying to remember how to spell *dialogue*. He'd failed most spelling tests since he was too cool to study.

Luckily, he'd stolen a powerful tool known as *Spell-check* from his last Author, and was now wielding its might over his manuscript.

"Like who?"

"My love interests, my best friends." He lifted his head to smile at her again. "You." Quickly, Blondie started mentally listing her ten favorite nail polish shades so her knees would stop wobbling. Darn him and his Author-given charm.

He raked a hand through his tousled mane, golden highlights (natural, of course—Heaven forbid Broody admit otherwise) and the soft locks shaded his vivid blue eyes.

"Fight Me Fuchsia, Blood of My Enemies Red," she muttered, desperately trying to retain her cool.

"Yeah, I think that's about it." He finished his list with a mention of his evil older brother.

In other words, he only knew successful characters. Those weren't the ones who needed this book most.

"Broody, have you ever been to the Deleted Files Hall?"

He shuddered. "No. Never."

All archetypes knew of it—a great and desolate hallway where characters, half-written and then deleted from pages, haunted those who still walked the pages of stories.

"Well, we're going." She leapt to his side, moving lightning-fast despite her high heels. Unlike a heroine, Blondie could slink, sprint, and seduce in her high heels from the very first page.

"C'mon." She tugged at Broody's arm until, with a mighty sigh, he stood and followed her.

They walked through the halls, which connected the rooms where most of the teen character archetypes lived. Blondie had tried to explore beyond her own hallway, but unless she was with a main character, like today, she always ended up back at her own front door, a circular route for a character with no arc. She relished the chance to see more of the massive building, and let her fingers trail along the cool stone walls, the air as crisp as the pages of a new novel.

Today, the setting was inspired by a castle, which explained why their clothing had magically changed to flowing robes. As they were both used to story-shifts, they didn't even blink at the sudden wardrobe changes. Although Broody did take a moment to twirl his cape dramatically.

"Dramatic." Blondie said, rolling her eyes.

"Always," he replied. "And, anyway, you're one to talk. How many times have you thrown dramatic temper tantrums just because I dumped you?"

"If I was given any character traits aside from jealousy and the obsessive need to be your girlfriend, maybe I'd be more rational," she replied, her words like ice, with small icicles hanging dangerously off the frozen punctuation.

They reached the Deleted Files Hall. "There." She pointed at the expanse in front of them, a long, dark corridor, with only a few lights throwing shadows in sharp relief against the gray stones.

Blondie wasn't quite sure exactly what that bit of exposition meant, but it certainly sounded cool.

Broody saw shades of supporting characters, each adorned with bits of personality and adjectival description, before their Authors had ruthlessly hit the DELETE button, sending them to their unfinished doom. Broody even recognized some of the slaughtered darlings surrounding him. There in the corner, was a teammate from one of his sportsball teams. And the ghost over to his right, that was his former love interest's cousin. Or sister. Or niece. He couldn't remember. Love interest's family were rarely given much page time, anyway.

"Go on." Blondie urged him, prodding him into the hall. "If you're going to write about being a main character, you should know what happens to those who fail to reach this goal."

The door slammed shut behind him, leaving him alone, and suddenly, the only POV character in this scene.

Not only did Blondie now have his book, but he was trapped in the hall with the deleted characters. Of course! How could he have trusted her? Why did he always fall for her tricks? Was it really the strawberry lip gloss? Perhaps there was a mind-melting magic attached to its scent?

As it was a medieval setting, Broody reached for his sword belt, but there was no weapon there. No! How would he defend himself? What could he possibly do to fend off these ghosts of stories unfinished?

"Stay back!" he called out. "Or I'll . . . I'll hit you with my very piercing stare!"

"Who are you?" one ghostly voice questioned.

"What do you want?" another asked, hauntingly.

"Why are you here?" the third phantomimed.

Broody shivered under the chilling, relentless barrage of ghoulish questions, to say nothing of the painfully obvious puns. No wonder these characters had been cut from their stories.

"I . . ." Broody tried to be the brave, brilliant, full-of-machismo hero he always naturally was. Somehow, he found this was getting harder to do, and he wasn't sure why. It just . . . wasn't coming easily to him anymore. It was as if the more words he put into the book, the less he felt like . . . well . . . like a Broody. "I'm here to help you! I want to ensure that everyone can become a main character!"

The ghostly voices whispered among themselves:

"Impossible!"

"Inconceivable!" That was from one character whose only discernible trait was never letting go of quoting *The Princess Bride*.

"Sacrebleu!" a third character, who spoke in the French their Author had learned in seventh grade, chimed in.

Broody waited for them to calm down again before he spoke. "I want to know why each of you was deleted, and then . . . then I'll be able to advise others. Help them. Ensure they never make your mistakes."

"We don't make mistakes!"

"*Je suis bon en français*," Frenchie said, and his friend patted him on the shoulder, sympathetic to his character flaw.

"No, no, not you!" Broody waved his hands, his eyebrows leaping like small, brown dancing caterpillars.

Drat. Even his similes had gotten less swoon-worthy lately.

"The Authors. They're the ones who make mistakes," he told them. And this, this he believed with every beat of his heart, which beat in his chest at quite a standard pace, unless he was meeting another love of his life. "Trust me. I've realized that."

Frenchie muttered an insult about *stupide* Authors.

"So, I'm working on this book to fix what Authors do."

For the next two hours, Broody did something he'd never done before. He listened. He carefully took notes on each character's flawed path. Some had been cut because their stories already had too many characters. Others were deleted for simply not being right for their roles. Still others had found their way to the Deleted Files Hall because their Authors had simply given up.

Broody had never before realized how lucky he'd been to possess such firm main character status. He was never deleted. Once in a while, he turned out to be a villain but, even then, he was always integral to the story.

It was so sad that a character could be cast aside so easily. They must not have tried hard enough. He'd be sure to write more in his book to fix that, ensuring that his readers would know all the tricks to remaining a popular character. Heck, it sounded like Frenchie listened to logic when a character called him out on his terrible French.

And main characters should never listen to logic.

Just as Broody finished jotting down a particularly good note to that effect, a new ghost appeared before him. "So, like, my Author was inspired by her totally righteous teen years in the eighties. Totally tubular, right?" The ghost adjusted his neon hat and sunglasses, flipping his mullet over his shoulder. "It's not my fault that kids these days can't embrace the gnarly awesomeness that is me."

Wait. Was that . . . a hair flip? And adjectives? Broody leaned forward. "What . . . what was your role in your novel?"

"Me? Take a chill pill, man! I was the freshest skater guy you'd ever met. A real bad-to-the-bone dude, who impressed all the bodacious ladies with my sweet kicks and rockin' fashion."

"You're wearing overalls and a crop top," Broody said.

"As if!"

"No, you most certainly are. I can see them. Shockingly, the neon hasn't burned my eyes yet."

"Whatever, dude. I'm just saying, I was the bad boy getting all the chicks in my sweet ride, till my Author decided I was outdated."

Broody dropped his notebook, coughed, and turned bright red. This . . . this strange, multicolored peacock of a man had once been a . . . bad boy? Perhaps even some strange version of Broody himself?

Surely not. Overalls? Neon? What self-respecting heartthrob would ever wear those?

And yet . . . The discarded character's mullet was incredibly luscious, and his eyes twinkled with the bright green-on-black of text on the first computer screens. Could it be true? This . . . this castoff had once been a Broody.

Until his Author had gotten tired of him.

Could my Author be tired of me . . . ? Broody wondered. *Also, am I using too many ellipses . . . ?*

It was almost, but not quite, enough to make him consider changing.

Eventually, the door opened, and Blondie peeked her head in. Her hair was now done up in some cool sci-fi headgear, which meant the setting must have shifted again outside. "Well," she asked, "did you learn anything?"

"If you use too many puns or eighties references, your Author will definitely cut you from the story."

Blondie sighed, the weight of the POV now settling again on her shoulders. It seemed, unfortunately, that her work wasn't done yet. Broody still failed to comprehend that other characters existed and had their own issues that were more complex than a bad cover photo.

It was time to employ an old trick guaranteed to make the narrative speed up.

She leaned in close, smiled charmingly at Broody . . . and hit him over the head with her futuristic designer purse, knocking him out.

Uh. Hello, dear readers. Sorry. Broody here. I can't exactly remember where I left off writing, and, quite frankly, rereading is not something I enjoy. Why would I reread a story when there are far more fascinating new stories ahead?

So, I'm going to jump into the next section. I may have promised to cover some other topic in earlier chapters, but I know you'll forgive me, right?

No?

Shall I remind you of my tragic backstory? Of how no one has ever loved me? How you are the only one who could ever possibly understand me?

Ah. There we go. I see you are now on my side.

CHAPTER 6

WHAT IF SOMEONE STOPS YOU FROM ACHIEVING YOUR DESTINY?

So now, thanks to my brilliant teaching, you've decided that you want to be a main character. Excellent. I knew you'd listen to me. The world would truly be a better place if every day at 2:00 p.m., the world gathered to listen to me and peer into my brilliant, sea-deep, star-bright, cerulean gaze. Can we make that happen?

You agree? Good. I knew I liked you.

Until the rest of the world signs on to the brilliant plan I like to call "Everyone Falls in Love with Me and Appoints Me as Leader of the Universe," I'll stick to giving you life advice.

We were discussing how some people may oppose your plan to become a main character. Surprisingly, not everyone wishes to be described with at least one hundred adjectives and featured on over a thousand book covers. Shocking, really.

Some of these people—antagonists—might even try to stop you from achieving your destiny! They'll confront you with things like "facts" and "strong logic" and "reality" in an attempt to quash your main character dreams.

Should you listen to these "rational" people?

Absolutely not.

I don't care what they have to say, or how many objections they have to the concept of a main character. Logic is for lesser characters, my budding protagonist flower. You run solely on a stronger substance . . . *drama*. Why, if I allowed myself to be stopped by anyone who quoted "facts" and "reality" at me, I would never have become a sixteen-year-old-rock-super-star-who-flies-his-own-helicopter-while-also-being-fluent-in-nineteen-lanugages.

So, if the haters try to get you down (That's still cool slang, right? Look. I'm a little worried about becoming . . . outdated, after a rather terrible run-in with some neon.) don't listen to them. You are a main character. I can sense it.

No, Broody, you cry, *they have so many good facts.*

False. One of the best parts of being a main character is that you get to ignore any fact you don't like.

For example, let's say I am a prince in medieval England. (Or really, any fantasy world, since we know that all fantasy worlds with medieval kingdoms are basically England.) I'd like to ride my horse to Paris to rescue a princess.

"But Prince Broodium," my page calls. "There is an ocean in the way!"

"That sounds like a clear and simple fact," I reply, reining in my stallion. "And, as such, I shall choose to ignore it completely."

And, thus, I happily gallop from London to Paris in under five paragraphs.

So, if someone presents you with cold, hard facts, hit them with an adjective-filled stare and ignore them completely. That's what I've always done, and it's never failed me.

Sure, a strange subset of readers known as "reviewers" have questioned the facts found in my books on a few occasions. But I think "reviewers" are just sad souls in search of true love. Maybe I should invite them all to prom.

Okay, but what if they try to stop you with more than just facts? What if they use the dreaded tool known as . . . *logic*?

This is a much trickier situation, to be sure, but nothing a main character can't handle. I've ignored logic countless times, no matter how often it's been presented to me. Why, I'd even hazard to say that the more logic offered, the more irrational my choices become.

Allow me, again, to illustrate.

I am invited to my love interest's Very Important violin recital. I'm already unpopular with her family, because they're incredibly jealous of how incredible I am (and, also, they think I'm sort of creepy and a bad influence on her, but that's beside the point). Anyway, my love interest states that I must attend this recital to prove my love.

But then plot happens, and I end up having to drive out of town to save the day. Because that's my main character job.

Now, logically, I should call my love interest.

Or text her.

Or post on any of her social media pages.

Perhaps my sidekick/best dude friend will even point these "logical" facts out to me. I will listen to his so-called logic, nod my head, maybe even clench my manly jaw. Then, I will say, "No communication. We handle this like men," and throw my phone out the window.

And you know what? My love interest will still eventually take me back. Even though the loss of my diamond-bright smile in the audience meant that she completely forgot how to play her instrument, threw it on the floor, and ran off in a shower of tears, thereby ruining her chance to gain entry into the music school of her dreams . . . Yeah, she'll still forgive me. Therefore, logic (and communication) are totally overrated.

Still worried that someone may push you to drop this whole main character quest? Don't worry.

Here are my three rules to use when dealing with anyone who is intent on stopping you from completing a goal:

1. Assume they are jealous.
2. Reassert that you are a main character.
3. Know that you are way better looking than them.

Let's go over those again, nice and slowly.

Always assume that someone trying to give you life advice is wrong and is also very jealous of you. Especially if that person is an adult. In novels, adults are always wrong. They'll give you bad advice like, "Hey, main character, maybe you should dump that creepy werelemur boyfriend of yours." Likewise, I firmly believe that all best friend supporting characters secretly wish they, too, were main characters. And what better way to become a main character than by removing your main character competition? Your "friends" secretly wish to have sparkling gemstone eyes, a devastating smile, and a thousand love interests pursuing them.

As for reasserting that you are a main character, that part is simple. All you have to do is say, very loudly, "My needs are more important than yours."

Voilà, you have established that the plot revolves around you.

It also never hurts to remind yourself that you are far, far better looking than anyone else. We've already established that certainty, as it's part of your main character identity, but maybe take a moment now to peer deeply into a mirror.

Please use the lines below to jot down a paragraph describing yourself in all your glorious beauty. Try to use at least seventeen adjectives and twelve adverbs.

_____

_____

_____

_____

_____

_____

Great. So now you have a handy list of all your awesomeness, as well as my three steps to ensure you will always be exactly as wonderful as that description ensures.

So, how would you put these steps into action?

I'll walk you through an example.

Let's say a so-called concerned best friend approaches you. Maybe it's a few chapters into your story and your plot is beginning to take shape. Your love interest has made some really excellent eye contact with you. Everything is going according to plan.

Until dreaded lunchtime.

It's a well-known fact that lunchtime lasts exactly long enough for a scene to occur. Lunchtime in certain schools can last several chapters.

At the lunch table, your best friend sits down across from you. Her one notable quirk is that she only eats orange food, so her tray is full of orange JELL-O, Cheetos, and . . . uh, oranges. (She may need a new quirk.)

"Hey, <NAME>," she says, her voice full of concern, her plain, average eyes swimming with . . . concern. "You . . . you shouldn't become a main character."

You narrow your eyes at her. This is a rather suspicious statement. Why would she say such a thing? Is it because you've ignored her for the last 111 pages? How selfish of her. Doesn't she know that you are a very busy main character, requiring a great deal of love and support from supporting characters whose sole reason for existing is to provide you support?

"But why?" you ask.

"Because it's dangerous," she says. She then explains how risky life as a main character can be, how she's concerned about how you've been skipping school to hunt evil monsters with your boyfriend, and how blah-blah-blah responsibility.

Is this because you make out with your love interest in front of her for hours on end? She shouldn't be mad about that—she'll get a love interest in, like, the third book. Or the thirteenth.

Perhaps she is incredibly jealous of you. That must be it. She wishes she was the one dating the werelemur prince of the night.

Ignore everything else she says, forever. Yes, even when she warns you it's a bad idea to tell the evil villain exactly where you've hidden the object that is your werelemur boyfriend's greatest weakness.

Remember. IGNORE ALL ADVICE ALWAYS.

(Unless it comes from me, in the context of this incredible book.)

Right. So, hopefully, those suggestions helped you. Never forget this chapter because a lot of people you meet simply will not understand how important it is to be a magnificent main character.

Speaking of ignoring logic, how about we do a little activity involving defying logic . . . and, well, me.

On the next page is a black-and-white portrait of my lovely visage. Will you please color me in with the most dreamy, impossible-in-real-life eye color? Then you should cut it out and keep it in your wallet, as a reminder that a main character's beauty may defy any logic you encounter.

We've covered deflecting questions and concerns from friends, but there are other forces in a main character's life who claim to be more concerned with "your best interest" and "your GPA" than how many adverbs your last lines of dialogue included.

Some people call these annoying and yet necessary beings *parents*.

I wouldn't know. I never had a childhood. I simply woke one morning, perfectly formed in my flawless nature as an immortal, handsome teenage main character.

Or did I?

I'll never tell.

Okay. I might tell you, but it will be in, like, eighteen sentences at least.

Let's get back to you.

Wow. That's a first for me. I hope I'm not turning into some bland Nice Guy Next Door. Note to self: Never move next door to any cute main characters with protagonist potential. Remain as far away as possible from them, while still finding ways to invade their personal space.

So, where were we? Oh, yes. Discussing your family's objections to you declaring your undying love for someone you've only known for thirteen seconds. Parents are so irrational. I don't understand why they can't believe in your undying love. I mean, it's not like you only caught a glimpse of your one true match for, like, two seconds. Thirteen seconds of intense gazing demonstrates some serious commitment.

Let's examine this situation in greater detail:

"Look," your concerned mother says. At least, I think she's concerned. I've never had a mother, and certainly never had a parent who expressed interest in my well-being, so it's confusing for me to imagine such a strange scenario. I'll discuss how this would go in my house in a moment.

Anyway, your mom says, "You can't possibly be in love with this brooding werelemur you just met."

"Mom! I love him!"

"You barely know him!"

"I love him!"

"You're sixteen."

"I love him!"

And so on and so forth. Really, no parent can actually argue with the "But I love him," response.

However, you might reply, "But you see, all I want is to be a main character."

Oh no. Now you've done it. You've caved and started using logic. That's . . . not good.

"I just wish you'd stick to being a supporting character."

"Eww, why?" you reply.

"Because, one, supporting characters' families are rather more stable and, well, alive than the families of main characters, and, two, supporting characters never become werelemurs or space princesses or baristas."

"Valid," you say, and manage to make an amazing comeback. "But they never get trilogies either."

Your mother considers this for a moment and finally says, "Fine. I accept this life choice, provided I can simply be mysteriously absent from your narrative, and not actually kidnapped or anything."

You agree to this plan and return to your pursuit of main character status.

There. Easily done.

As for me . . . Reader, I must confess. I . . . I did have a childhood. Once. Er. I may have also confessed this earlier, but for drama's sake, let's just pretend this is the very first time you're learning this most shocking information.

You see, I was not born to be a protagonist. Nor even a supporting character. I was born a . . . villain. My family line has always been full of morally gray, complex characters who fans adore, despite the numerous terrible acts we've done—probably because we're so ridiculously good-looking.

Let me take you back to the moment in my life when everything changed.

No, not the time we first gazed longingly at each other, though don't worry, that will always remain a beautiful, glittering moment in my mind. (Just . . . uh . . . don't ask me your name.)

I mean the moment that I, too, achieved main character status.

It was a stormy day—as stormy as my ultramarine eyes, as turbulent as the turmoil in my heart. We were in our castle/mansion/edifice-of-affluent-evilness, when my father found me. He, like me, is very handsome. Unlike me, he is an adult, and also evil.

"Broody," my father said. "It is time. Embrace your destiny."

"No!" I cried defiantly, my brilliant eyes burning with self-righteous passion.

"You must," he growled back, his voice like gravel and his gaze as stony as granite. "You must become a villain, as we all have for time immortal."

"Never!" I cried, and ran outside into the rushing wind, allowing the air to tousle my hair fetchingly for me. How could I be a villain when I was destined for so much more? *I am clearly hero material, aren't I?* I thought in weighty internal monologue, which was as heavy as the parental responsibilities my evil father tried to lay on my strong, manly, muscular shoulders.

A little voice whispered to me, and it sounded like my father, reminding me of the long line of evil overlords from which I descend.

I blocked out the urges, determined not to listen. Determined to become a . . . a main character. No one would stop me. I would become the main-est of all main characters, the most pro of all protagonists.

I clenched my fist in the pouring rain. (When did it start raining? Directly when I started experiencing these intense emotions, of course.)

I made my vow that day, and I have never wavered from my path.

So, if I was able to cast my troubled past aside and change myself, embracing my own main character destiny, then you, too, can surely become one. We both have obstacles to overcome. I was a ridiculously attractive evil character, and you are a real, live, flesh-and-bones human who wishes to be transformed into a figure of fiction. Don't let that stop you.

There's one more situation I'd like to discuss. And it's a tricky one.

What if you feel yourself being demoted to a . . . supporting character role? This is bad—like, really, *really* bad—but it's best to be prepared.

First, familiarize yourself with the warning signs of this terrible condition:

1. **The novel is in multiple POVs:**
   Some novels head-hop from one character to another. These books are often enjoyable as a main character, as the reader gets to not only learn your own thoughts on how awesome you are, but also read other characters reflecting on your awesomeness.
   However, there is an inherent danger when there is more than one POV—someone else's viewpoint could be more compelling than yours.

2. **The novel uses a framing story:**
   Quick, check your first chapter. Are you a character who is an experienced storyteller or, perhaps, you are entering a theater to

watch a dramatic production?

You, my friend, are in *grave* danger! For the love of all that is Broody, stop speaking or turn around immediately! Otherwise, you may find that the secondary story—the tale you're spinning for the prince, or the romance playing out on the stage—is the actual focus of the book. You'll only appear once more, in the closing chapter, where you'll soon be forgotten.

3. **You get kidnapped:**
Unlike the previous items in this list, this plot device has nothing to do with the way the Author chose to set up the story, and everything to do with your lack of agency as a character. Remember our discussion about agency? Being kidnapped (or fainting for any extended period of time) is the worst thing that can happen when you don't have it. The plot will continue on without you, while you're trapped, waiting for someone else to come to your rescue.

4. **You have a really, really cool best friend (who you're not romantically interested in at all):**
It seems like you might be the protagonist of the story. After all, it's in your POV and you've landed some really great adjectives. But wait! There is also a really, really cool best friend in this story. It quickly becomes apparent that your only role is to narrate the exciting events that happen to your best friend. You are nothing more than a human video camera, recording and saving

these cool moments that are occurring to someone else. Heck, your so-called friend's name might even be on the cover of the book.

(And for the record, Gatsby wasn't that great. Mediocre, maybe.)

So, what do you do if you notice any of these things happening?

First of all, PANIC.

Seriously.

Throw the most epic meltdown possible. Incite your fans to riot. Remind the Author of your awesomeness by haunting her dreams.

Complain about it on Twitter.

Other than that . . . Nope. I've got no other advice.

Job Applications: Only Protagonists Need Apply

As we've already covered, some people may question your main character lifestyle. They'll say you're pigeonholing yourself—you won't have a role to fill in other stories. That you're useless and overdramatic.

That's, in part, because supporting characters have it easier in one aspect of their development: they always know what they're supposed to do. If you're the comedic relief, you're going to get your moment to shine whenever the Author decides the reader needs a laugh. If you're a teacher, well, your sole purpose is to teach the main characters something seemingly insignificant, which will only be recalled when they are facing certain doom. Otherwise, you might not even have lines.

Main characters, however, can fill any number of roles. Because I am so magnanimous, I've included some recent applications for main character roles, to show you how limitless your possibilities can be:

Job Posting: Chosen One in Hiding

This role is for any princess/warrior/otherwise-destined-Chosen One who has no idea of his or her true identity.

Candidates should possess powers they don't understand, a deep moral code, and a cheerful disposition, despite being sent to an orphanage as a small child.

NOTE: Please only apply for this position if you are absolutely sure you are not the Chosen One. The successful applicant must be able to state with full certainty that we picked the wrong person for at least the first fifty pages.

Tasks:

• Save the day.

• Avenge your parents.

• Rule the kingdom. Despite your having absolutely no interest nor any experience in political maneuvering, we do hope by the end of the book you will be able to handle ruling a kingdom with no preparation or assistance.

Required Experience:
None, please. We want the Chosen One to learn all skills through the magic of plot or through actual magic. However, we won't discourage dormant skills, buried deep within your amnesiac memory to reappear if it makes things easier.

To Apply:
Applications are considered on a rolling basis, as each new season brings a new lovable orphan to court. Please be prepared with your best curtsy and meaningful piece of jewelry. If you can capture a love interest before you reach the palace, that may also prove helpful.

Job Posting: Improbably Talented Small-Town Teen

Great new job posting! Perfect for any teens with far more talent than would be possible at their age, especially if their talents are highly plot relevant. Are you capable of piloting a submarine *while* playing the trombone? Perfect! Have you memorized every single one of Shakespeare's plays, and filmed yourself as all the characters? Even better.

All we need from you is to have some highly specific skills, with only the vaguest sense of how you got those skills.

Tasks:

• Sharpen your weird skills even more with specific quests that seem oddly perfect for your skill set.

• Use said skills to find love/save the world/get into college.

Required Experience:
Must be from a small town. No city kids need apply.

To Apply:
We'll come to you with a highly specific contest that only you could win.

Job Posting: "Great White Savior"

Are you a bland, Caucasian main character? Well, we've got a vaguely offensively stereotyped PoC nation in our fantasy world that needs you to save them.

Tasks:

• Find the nation.

• Marvel at how incredibly strange and outdated their quirky customs are.

• Learn their ways.

• Take over.

Required Experience:

The ideal candidate will have a very strong ego, the unwavering certainty that his nation's way of doing things is the best and only way, and absolutely no sensitivity for others' cultures.

An ability to charm locals into providing them with religious and magical talismans is highly desired.

The ideal candidate needs to be able to fluently learn entire languages in the span of three paragraphs.

To Apply:

Strike out on your own, confident in your own colonialism-imbued strengths. We are sure you will find a country that needs saving soon.

Job Posting: Reluctant Leader of the Rebellion

Have you ever wanted to overthrow the evil over-lords oppressing you? No? What if they kidnapped that one family member you care about most?

Aha! We knew you'd be interested.

Tasks:

• Lead a ragtag team against a far larger, better-equipped army of bad guys.

• Deploy complex maneuvers and guerrilla warfare combat skills.

• Offer rousing, morale-boosting speeches that will bring your troops to the brink of tears.

• Have at least one romantic liaison with someone in your squadron (who will likely die, but then you can make a rousing speech in your loved one's memory).

• Dramatically faint in battle.

Required Experience:

None. We prefer our military leaders fresh from a small farm town or other backwater locale. We trust that your main character skills will sufficiently prepare you for the use of any and all weapons and the development and deployment of winning battle tactics.

To Apply:
Please state loudly and clearly for all to hear that the rebellion isn't your problem and that you are just trying to survive. This will ensure that something terrible will happen to your loved ones, allowing us to offer you the position.

Job Posting: Overthrowing the Patriarchy

Don't you hate how there are all those things that guys can do, but girls can't?

In a contemporary, this might be a certain sport. In fantasy, it's just about everything. Except needlework—girls are always allowed to do needlework—and that's exactly why you hate it.

Well, rather than focusing your efforts on improving the entire world for all women or ensuring that traditionally feminine traits and roles are still respected by the narrative, we'd prefer for a white, able-bodied, cishet, media-standard-approved beautiful female to become a feminist icon. (Just, you know, not the intersectional type. It is well known that a character can only represent one group at a time.)

This role will require our chosen heroine to sneak into a male-dominated activity, such as fencing, football, or, more generally, existing, and show off her awesome skills in order to prove that women are just as capable as men.

Provided they're, you know, pretty, privileged, culturally dominant, conventional women.

Tasks:

- Insult other women. A quick "Ugh, I'm not like other girls" is preferred, but we will accept angry tirades, too.

- Befriend a boy who excels at the hobby the candidate is attempting to infiltrate. Try not to fall in love with him, even though it is inevitable.

- Make no female friends, step on the achievements of all those who came before you without acknowledging their contributions (especially if they are women of color), and refuse to teach any other women how to do this task for which you've struggled so hard to gain recognition.

Required Experience:
A long history of being annoyed by your "girlish, silly" sister/best friend/rest of womankind should do the trick nicely. Although not always required, it would be helpful if the applicant is able to easily disguise herself as a young man for greater ease of sneaking into the boys-only club and, as a bonus, making her love interest question his sexuality. This may require cutting one's hair and wearing boys' clothes, and nothing else.

To Apply:
Fill out a form that states, "I, <YOUR NAME HERE>, am not like other girls and wish to overthrow the patriarchy, but only in a very specific, self-serving way."

Please ensure that the paper is not pink, scented, or otherwise "girly" in any way, shape, or form.

Job Posting: Becoming That Thing You Hate (Like a Popular Girl or a Pop Star)

Do you have strong opinions about a certain role in life? Perhaps you hate the popular kids, finding them vain and vapid. Or maybe you cannot stand pop music and wish to return to the days of good music . . . like anything from the '80s.

Well, we'd like to hire you to become that very thing you can't stand.

Tasks:

• Begin the story with the best of intentions.

• Slowly morph into the very thing you swore you would never become.

PLEASE NOTE: We do allow for flexibility with your realization. Feel free to either come to understand that people are as awful as you thought they were and change back to your original state. Alternatively, accepting and embracing your new way of life is also considered acceptable.

Required Experience:

Depending on that which you do not wish to become, some prior experience may be required. For example, if you wish to apply for the "I Always Wanted to Become a Successful Actress but Now I've Realized

Everyone in Hollywood Is Shallow and Vapid" track, we request that you have at least one prior acting role, no matter how small.

To Apply:
Accidentally become part of a posse of people or gain a boyfriend who will influence your rather malleable personality. One or the other should have the necessary application.

Job Posting: Agreeing to an Arranged Marriage

Are you a princess? No? Would you like to be one? Well, we've got a great opportunity for you. You're getting married off to a total stranger!

That's right. Just write back to this job posting and we'll pair you with some powerful character you've never met before in your life.

Tasks:

• Declare adamantly you won't fall in love with him.

• Fall in love with him anyway.

Required Experience:
Must be good at dancing. There will inevitably be at least one ball.

To Apply:
Turn sixteen. Wait for a royal decree.

Blondie here.

Yeah, I snuck in with another note.

I'm not here to explain Broody for once. Because those job applications? Those are un-explainable. I can't believe him. Are those really the only things he thinks main characters can do?

I don't know about you, reader, but I'm not trying to achieve main character status just to be some problematic savior character.

I've listed a couple of job ideas below. Maybe you can nudge your Author toward one of them?

Leader of a diverse, intersectional group of badasses:
You, as a hero, must balance your own talents with the incredible skills of an intersectional group of other cool characters.

Protector of your own (non-European) culture:
You protect your family's traditions and way of life against yet another obnoxious, pro-colonialism so-called hero.

Self-Saving Princess:
You're strong, competent, and successful. You don't need a dude to rescue your kingdom from evil. You've got this.

Leader of a Necessary Rebellion:
Unlike a rebellion based solely on giving Broody a chance to take his shirt off, this calls for a hero who is politically savvy, brave, and ready to persist until positive change occurs.

What do you think? Aren't those *way* better? Yeah, of course they are. I'm always right. At least until the turning point of the book. Comes with the whole "being evil" package.

As for turning points . . . Oh, I'm sure Broody will cover them. Eventually. Once he stops complimenting his biceps.

xoxo, B

Don't Give Up, Because That's Just Silly

Perhaps none of those job descriptions sound very appealing to you. Maybe you don't feel you have enough main character traits to actually pursue such a position. Or maybe an antagonist has already attempted to foil your pursuit of your chosen destiny.

Whatever the case may be, you might be feeling like this quest is going to be a challenge for you.

Believe me. It's okay to feel that way. Every main character has moments where he or she feels like giving up. Granted, none of us actually *do* give up. We'd be pretty awful main characters, then.

So I'm going to remind you not to give up either.

How would you get out of these bleak situations? Provide a two to three sentence response to each.

You've been kidnapped. Your love interest might be planning a rescue. . . . But the son of the evil over-lord is also pretty good-looking. Oh. And the world is going to end tomorrow if you don't escape.

_____

_____

Someone stole your band's song for Battle of the Bands! It's only five minutes until you have to go on stage, and your floppy-haired guitarist, far-too-loud drummer, and totally unnecessary tambourine girl are in need of your guidance.

_____

_____

Your love interest has disappeared, after you two failed to communicate, yet again. You only have a few hours until you leave for outer space/summer camp/Kansas.

_____

_____

You've been invited to a very fancy formal dance, but you have nothing to wear! Armed with only your personality, a chapter's worth of adjectives, and hope. What will you do?

_____

_____

Those were some great answers! Well done. Now, just in case that little pop quiz has you doubting if you really want to be a main character, I've made a list of lots of awesome things only main characters get to have:

1. **Your emotions control the weather.**
   Have you ever tried to be happy on a rainy day? It's pretty difficult. The weather is all gloomy, the storm-cloud-gray sky reminds you of my eyes . . .
   Anyway, worry no longer.
   As a main character, your emotions will always reflect the weather.

2. **Things come easier for you.**
   That might sound silly, since you're currently mired in a quest that feels impossible. But as a main character, certain things in life are just . . . easier. For example, you never have to shout, "What?" at a crowded concert. Everyone will always hear you perfectly. And you'll never burn your tongue on hot coffee or get bitten by a mosquito or run out of toilet paper. These embarrassing things simply don't happen to main characters.

3. **Your life follows an orderly pattern.**
   You'll wake up, go to school, save the world, come home, and never miss a single moment of beauty sleep. Everything will proceed along a track, where each event builds on the previous one. Events will move from first meeting to first kiss to first date to first time you battle zombies together in a regimented schedule that makes sense. Unlike in real life, where you could have eight different first kisses and no dates, or have to take a test *without* an amazing study montage first.

4. **The only bad things that happen to you are plot-related**.
   Don't worry. You'll never trip and fall in a puddle or forget your homework, unless it has important bearing on the plot. I cannot promise you a completely happy,

misfortune-free path as a main character, but I can guarantee that you will grow and learn from each bad experience that happens to you along the way.

Unlike me. I am incapable of learning from my mistakes.

5. **You'll pick up new skills quickly.**
Speaking of learning, one of the coolest perks of being a main character is how quickly you'll be able to grasp new skills. Ever want to learn a new language? As a main character, you'll become fluent as fast as your Author can type your dialogue into Google Translate. Need to scale a mountain? Don't worry. One quick lesson on rock climbing and you'll be good to go.

6. **Most injuries are mild.**
Aside from plot-related medical events such as amnesia, you'll never get little bumps, scrapes, or even concussions when you should. You'll never even have calluses on your hands. Likewise, your physical size won't stop you from being badass. If you're a girl, you'll be short and slender, yet capable of wielding a massive battle-ax if that's what's required of you. Pretty sweet.

Maybe these reasons aren't enough to win you over. That's okay. You can take a little rest. You know what? We've spent a lot of quality time together already, and I am absolutely sure you have what it takes to be a main character.

Even on days when it doesn't feel like you do.

NARRATIVE INTERLUDE: WHILE OUR DAZZLING HERO DREAMS, EVIL TAKES A WELL-DESERVED BREAK

Broody found himself in his bed, with a throbbing headache, and only the faintest memory of how he'd gotten there. Had Blondie . . . knocked him out? And then dragged him all the way back?

In four-inch heels?

The girl was strong, he'd give her that.

His gaze flicked over to his desk. He wondered if she'd given the book back. Or if he should get back to writing it. But . . . sleep was good. And he was tired. Surely he'd be able to finish it tomorrow. How hard could it be to write a book?

Easy. Far easier than being a character in a book. He let his eyes flutter closed, practicing for when he'd next need to flutter his impossibly long eyelashes, and then sleep claimed him.

He was just settling into a lovely dream where his trilogy was being made into a four-part movie series, when he was awakened by a soft voice.

"Brooooooody," the voice called. "Oh, Master Fitzbroodum H. Trouserton."

He blinked. No one had called him that name in ages.

When he opened his eyes, a figure hovered in front of him, faint, wearing a historical gown that actually seemed . . . accurate, with white flowing waves of fabric falling gently to the floor. Her hair was pinned elaborately on top of her head and she had a quill and notebook tucked under one arm.

"Who are you?" Broody blearily asked, rubbing his eyes to clear his vision.

"I am the Ghost of Authors Past," she said simply.

He rolled his eyes. A *retelling*. Wonderful. Now he'd have to act like he'd never read the original.

Then again, he hadn't. But he had watched the Muppet version.

"What do you want?"

"I want to give you a lesson on the history of fiction."

"What? I thought I was in a short story, not a textbook," Broody called.

"I'll be concise," she promised.

He derisively snorted with derision, which was a complex form of disbelief and scorn. "I'm a main character. I don't need a lesson."

"Are you sure about that?"

"Uh. *Yeah.* I've been starring in novels for yeaaaaaars." He tried not to think about the strange, mulleted, neon-ed young hero he'd met in the Deleted Files Hall. That guy had probably starred in plenty of books in his day, too . . . and had never guessed his fate.

Around them, the moonlight streaming into the room rippled like water on the floor, but unlike water, it could not show his reflection. Stupid moonlight.

The ghost folded her arms and peered down at him. "Broody, literature has evolved over the course of centuries. You can't simply decide to write a book in a day."

"Why not?" He tried to melt her with his most vivid smile, but it seemed she was un-meltable. It had to be because she was a ghost. Not that she just wasn't interested in Broody. "I'll follow the rules, I promise."

"What rules?"

"You know, the main character rules. The plot rules. All that stuff that happens in every book."

The ghost rolled her eyes more magnificently than any character he'd ever seen. Well, she did have centuries of haunting for practice. "Broody, that's just the problem! Those rules are constantly changing. You can't just pick some version of them and act like they're law. Why, it was a woman who invented the horror genre when Mary Shelley got sick of all the drama and decided to write *Frankenstein*."

"Who would get sick of drama? That's my favorite thing."

She gave him a death-glare that, had she been alive, would have been terrifying. As it was, he discounted her. Because she was a ghost.

And also a woman.

"Although I represent all writers of the past, I want you to know I especially represent women writers whose work has been continually lambasted, ignored, and pushed aside in favor of elevating the male narrative."

"Well, that's 'cause the male narrative is pretty damn awesome." Broody smirked. "Am I right, or am I, like, super-duper right?"

That earned him another eye roll. Really, this lady ghost-Author should just be grateful to have a few minutes of speaking time in his story. He was being incredibly generous about the whole thing.

"Look, as a man, you have historically gotten to star in movies and books. Not only is it much harder for women to be cast in leading roles, it's even harder for women of color and those of diverse, marginalized identities. They get way less main character access than you have. Just as I, Author of the past, began to challenge the narrative by including more diverse characters, I hope you'll remember this information when advising people about being main characters."

"That sounds like a lot of work," Broody replied.

"Yes. Writing *is* a lot of work," the Author agreed, "but it is the very best kind of work. The life-changing kind."

She handed him a notebook. "Here. A gift from the past. Use it well, and remember the power and responsibility writers have."

Broody shoved the notebook under his pillow. He didn't need a new one. He was writing his book in a notebook with a mirror taped to the front, so he could always remember his inspiration for writing in the first place.

He had only slept a few minutes when a new figure appeared over him. This being, too, was a ghostly being, but dressed in modern clothing—a T-shirt with a witty saying about writing, jeans, and fluffy bunny slippers. The spirit held a steaming cup of ghostly coffee in one transparent hand. Broody hadn't even known ghosts drank coffee, but he supposed it helped them with all these late-night hauntings.

The new apparition said, "I'm the Ghost of Authors Present."

"Oh?" Broody raised a perfectly manicured eyebrow. "Author's present? Please, give it to me. I love gifts!"

"No, Authors, plural; Present, period of time." She glared at him through her glasses. "Learn your grammar! And please, stop being mean to the poor comma. It's downright afraid of you by now."

"I love the comma," he replied. "It's got great flair. It's like a cool tattoo for words."

She just shook her head. "Oh, Broody. You're a pain." Her coffee steamed up toward the ceiling, twisting into shapes that Broody thought looked a little like hearts.

Hearts were his second favorite shape, after triangles.

"But I'm your favorite pain. We've had so many blockbusters together. When do I get to be in another movie with vampires and werelemurs?"

"Actually . . ." She sighed, as if she might have bad news to tell him.

He froze like a frozen thing, trapped on an ice-cold frozen lake. "What?"

"Broody." She repeated his name. "I think . . . I think it's time you realized there's a lot more to your chosen age range of books than werelemurs."

He smiled. "You're right. There're wizards, and dystopian regimes, too."

"No, Broody." And now she sounded like a teacher. He usually ignored teachers, so he had to try extra hard to make sure he was listening. "Werelemurs, wizards, dystopian regimes . . . all those things are old, tired YA trends. The subject matter of young adult literature keeps growing and changing and breaking new ground."

He stared up at her, confused. "But why?"

"Because that's what books do. They change. They can change readers, too."

"I never change, though." He tapped his chest. "Me, I'm always Broody. I'm reliable." He paused. "Well, not *actually* reliable, because you know I hate showing up to places on time. But I am reliably unreliable, right?"

She ruffled his hair like he was a puppy. "Maybe someday you'll change, Broody. Someday."

He shook his head. Change was scary. Change happened to other characters, not him.

He looked up at the present Author, and for the first time, he realized she sounded a little bit like Blondie, if Blondie sounded more like a main character, and less like an evil person. Which was strange to think about. Blondie had been a villain for as long as he'd known her. Even when they'd dated, it had always been in the backstory, never part of the actual narrative.

The Author said, "Ah, well. My main task is simply to remind you that there are many, many books in the world with many, many stories to tell. Do you think you can remember that when you wake up?

"Of course. I remember everything."

"Broody," she said in a warning tone of voice.

"I do!"

"What are the names of your last three love interests?"

"Uh . . ." He rubbed his chin. "Um. My Heart, Babe, and Sweetheart."

The Author patted his head. "I'll write a memo for you. A little better than trusting your memory."

"Wait! Oh! One of them was '*mi querida*,' he said, waggling his eyebrows. "I was very romantic."

"No. Your Author found that word on Google Translate." She paused, as if to give him another lecture, but decided against it. Which was good, because Broody's brain was already overloading with all this character development being shoved at him. He was quite sure steam was leaking from his ears, just like from her coffee cup. "Good night, Broody."

When Broody fell back asleep, he dreamed of strange stories where he wasn't the star. He didn't like it, and woke with a start.

A little while later, a third visitor appeared. Young— younger than even a teenager might be. "Hiya, Broodster," he said cheerily, jumping on the foot of Broody's bed.

Annoyed, Broody looked at the small boy. "I only have to tolerate small children in stories where I need to show off my babysitting skills. Go away."

"I can't." The kid smiled down at Broody. "I'm the Ghost of Authors Future."

"Great. Yeah, yeah, I'll remember how important literature is and how great teens are, and blah blah blah. Now let me get some sleep."

The boy bopped Broody on the forehead. "Don't patronize me just because I'm younger than you."

"That's an awfully big word for a little kid," Broody replied.

The kid shrugged. "I'm an Author. We know lots and lots of words."

Finally, Broody sat up, ready to pay attention to what he hoped would be the last visitor of the night. The child had some sort of fancy new computer/ smartphone/tech thingie, which Broody didn't even bother looking at. Thanks to the publishing gods, his technology was always out of date by the time his book came out.

"Right, so"—the kid finished tapping on the screen—"I'm supposed to talk to you about why young adult literature matters so much."

"Uh, because it gets mega-big blockbuster deals, duh," Broody said.

"No, silly." The kid laughed. "Also, your slang is out of date."

"Well, it's not my fault. I'm always out of date. A book can take years to publish," Broody countered, feeling a little embarrassed.

"That's true. But what's more important is the content of those books."

"Don't worry! I plan to tell my future main characters all about how important adjectives are."

The young Author shook his head, his dark hair flopping into his eyes.

Cute kid, really, Broody thought. He wondered if it would be worth describing the Author, if the fan-artists would just whitewash him, like they did to lots of characters.

"No. I need you to talk about . . ." He paused, said the word carefully. "Probab . . . probs . . . ah! Problematic content in books."

"That's a really big word. I'm not sure I can spell it." Broody tried to compliment the kid, while stealthily trying to learn exactly what the word meant. "Could you use it in a sentence?"

"When your only person of color is not only a supporting character, but also gets killed off to advance your goals, Broody, that's problematic."

"Ahh, I see." He rubbed his chin, but did not actually understand Kid Author's point. "I will try my best to make sure that doesn't happen anymore. As long as it doesn't, you know, involve a lot of work. Or me changing. I like myself exactly the way I am."

The Kid Author shook his head and jumped down from the bed. "Sometimes, things have to change to get better, Broody."

And then the boy vanished.

In the morning, Broody made himself coffee, which he drank black, like his dark, mysterious past, and poured himself a bowl of cereal, which he preferred to be as sugary and artificial as his romantic future.

And then, he found a memo:

DEAR BROODY:

You have been visited by three ghosts.

They had lots of good advice.

Please listen to them.

P.S. Start learning your love interests' names, dingbat!

Wow. Three different Authors had all told him he might need to change. That was just weird. Well, the fact that it happened three times wasn't weird. Stuff always happened to main characters in threes.

After another moment of thought, he decided to pretend that the dreams hadn't happened. He had a book to write.

And yet . . .

He went and grabbed the notebook from the Ghost of Authors Past.

CHAPTER 7

PUTTING ALL THE PARTS TOGETHER

So I have some yummy genre and setting all picked out for you, most lovely reader. Now it's time to explain some common events that occur within stories. Think of this as a road map for your journey along your main character path. Yes, your Author's going to be crafting the story, that's true, but . . . Authors are kind of clueless. Sometimes they even talk to us characters. If an Author starts chatting you up, why not guide them into writing you a better story?

```
F  S  V  C  V  B  Y  C  X  H  R  R  I  C  G        PROTAGO
L  W  O  D  A  B  S  J  J  S  O  R  A  S  H        HERO
I  S  C  E  N  E  B  K  W  Y  H  L  N  G  O        BROODY
J  W  V  A  M  E  G  A  H  M  P  T  T  G  R        PLOT
N  P  G  B  X  A  Q  Z  H  B  A  F  A  Q  E        ALLUSION
K  T  Y  N  E  A  C  B  V  O  T  I  G  Q  H        ADJECTIV
O  T  E  I  R  O  N  Y  B  L  E  M  O  W  B        METAPHO
Q  T  N  O  I  S  U  L  L  I  M  S  N  A  E        ANTAGON
Q  O  C  Y  D  O  O  R  B  S  Q  L  I  F  E        FLASHBA
A  L  L  U  S  I  O  N  N  M  U  H  S  Z  Y        IRONY
S  E  G  K  F  U  X  P  Z  O  Z  O  T  R  H        ILLUSION
G  S  T  S  I  N  O  G  A  T  O  R  P  O  B        CHASE
M  A  Q  K  F  E  U  A  Q  M  T  O  L  P  Y        SCENE
N  H  K  C  A  B  H  S  A  L  F  A  F  T  C        CAMEO
J  C  E  V  I  T  C  E  J  D  A  Y  M  C  F        SYMBOLIS
```

Before I jump into the parts of the story, I'd like to talk a little bit about common elements that can be included in a book. Think of the parts of a story as clothing. You can't very well walk around without a shirt. Well, unless you're me. We all know my shirt is an optional piece of clothing, especially on book covers.

The items below are more like accessories—corsages for prom or the really expensive earrings I gave you to show you how much wealthier I am than that Nice Guy Next Door who actually cares about what you think, or that tiara you have even though you're an orphan and have no idea why you'd have it. They decorate your story.

We've already discussed POV on page 50, so now I'm going to talk about the types of voice you might find in a story. These can exist in any type of POV, and influence what words the Author chooses to write:

Active Voice

Action happens in a dramatic, easy-to-read way. Active voice uses tons of verbs which show action, and is preferred by most readers and editors.

EXAMPLE: Broody saved the day.

Passive Voice

In this style of writing, the Author tells, rather than shows, all the fun of the story. Passive voice uses an overabundance of "to be" verbs, like *is*, *was*, or *are*. Usually, your readers don't like this as much. They say it puts them to sleep. I say they've just spent too long gazing upon my majesty and need to rest their eyes.

EXAMPLE: The day was saved by Broody.

Passive-Aggressive Voice

This is the way I prefer to tell a story. It allows me to subtly insult whoever I chose.

EXAMPLE: Why would you even think anyone besides Broody could save the day?

Aside from voice, there are plenty of other tools Authors use to decorate your story. Tell your Author to get creative and use as many of them as possible.

Plot Twists

When something unexpected happens, causing the story to take a dramatic turn.

EXAMPLE: You meet me and think I'm a jerk, mainly because I glare at you, make fun of you, and then ignore you for two weeks. PLOT TWIST. I am actually madly in love with you, but an evil witch has told me if I ever kiss you, the entire world will catch on fire.

But I'm also still kind of a jerk. That's not the plot twist. Just the, uh, curse part.

Dream Sequences

When part of the story occurs within a character's dream. Oftentimes, the reader is not aware the character is dreaming until after it's over. Sometimes, the dream might impact the plot, providing a clue to a mystery that the main character couldn't solve while awake. Other times, it's just there to look cool.

EXAMPLE: Our story opens with a thrilling dragon-versus-dragon race, through twisting canyons and over vast, fantastic forests, where every leaf on every tree is actually a butterfly. This world is majestic, beautiful, and vivid.

Then an alarm clock goes off, startling the main character awake, and she begins her day in boring, average Cleveland, where there are no dragons and no magic trees. As much as the main character hopes that the cool dragon dream sequence happened because she is destined to become a dragon rider and escape her dull life, she soon realizes the Author had no good reason for that scene.

Other than the fact that flying dragons are cool.

Flashbacks

A bit like dream sequences, as they disrupt the flow of the actual story. However, unlike dream sequences, this event actually happened to the character. Usually, it reveals a useful piece of backstory the reader would not otherwise learn.

EXAMPLE: As the most popular guy in school, I mock and tease everyone less cool than me. This is rather annoying to you, as you happen to be friends with some of the least cool people I've ever met. Just when the reader is about to give up on me being a remotely decent human, *bam,* flashback.

Suddenly, the reader is submerged in a memory of me as a middle schooler when someone laughed at me for having the hiccups.

Just as suddenly, the story returns to the present day, and the reader is overcome with sympathy for the embarrassment I suffered.

P.S. "Flash-forwards" are similar, but as they show the future, I don't really like them. I want my readers to be surprised that I've married my one true love!

Irony

This is something to do with an iron, I think? To make my clothes nicely pressed for prom?

Oh, no. Wait! I've just remembered the definition (or perhaps consulted the dictionary Blondie threw at me). For stories, let's focus on dramatic irony, which is when the reader knows something the characters do not. For example, let's say I've saved all my pennies for a lovely gift for my girlfriend, but she has accidentally poisoned herself.

Gah! Wait. I muddled two examples.

EXAMPLE ONE: I see my girlfriend lying next to me in a tomb, and she looks like she's dead. Although the audience knows she's merely taken a highly plot-convenient sleeping potion, I am not rational enough to consider this as a possibility. Therefore, I take my own life in dramatic fashion. That's a bad move.

The other example is very long and boring and involves something super-stupid called "selfless love," so I'm not going to discuss any gifts, even if they come from Magi. Whoever they are. I bet they're werelemur hunters or something.

Selfless love. Ugh. Waste of time.

Allusion

When another story is referred to. I've used this many times within this book, but in a very stealthy manner, so as to not offend any Authors, or make them swoon. That being said, there's a magnificent example of an allusion in the definition above this one.

Illusion

Something that you think exists, but actually doesn't! (Like your agency in this story.)

NOT A LITERARY DEVICE, BROODY

Foil

Another character (who can be any of the supporting characters I've already described) who makes your own characterization more vivid by being your opposite. They're sometimes your sidekick or your antagonist's best friend or your teammate. They're never your love interest (except in fan fiction).

Chase Scene

We chase something. For a whole scene. It's exciting! (And great filler if the Author doesn't know what to write next.)

Pet the Dog

A moment where the reader gains sympathy for your villain because they do something nice.

My favorite moments, to be honest. It's almost like I get to be a real person for a scene.

Hand Wave

The Author will use this tool to explain away any inconsistencies in the story. For example: We main characters are able to race across all of Manhattan in a thrilling car chase, never once encountering traffic or running over a tourist. The Author handwaves it away by saying that the traffic was unusually light that day . . . and all the tourists are watching some musical about the founding fathers, anyway.

Cameo

When a character from another one of the Author's books appears for a moment. This can also be a continuity nod, which means that it shows how this book is related to the other books in the Author's series. Me? I'm just annoyed the Author has books that don't feature me.

Really Cool Line

Exactly what it sounds like. Maybe it's my catch-phrase. Or my favorite magical attack. Whatever it is, the Author will use it at least ninety times in one book.

That Thing We Discuss but Never See

Ah yes. You know that time . . . with the frying pan . . . and the tap dancers? Yeah! That!
    A.K.A.
    We characters know a thing that we'll never tell the readers. And we like it that way.

Symbolism

One of my all-time favorites! This one can be used so many different ways. See, Authors exist in a place they call The Real World, which is a drab and yet strangely unpredictable land. In this land, they've gotten used to certain images or visual cues meaning more than they actually do.

EXAMPLE ONE: If you and I decide to sit in a swan-shaped boat for a lovely river cruise, you know we're going to share a romantic moment. In The Real World, swan boats are a super-important sign of true love.

EXAMPLE TWO: If someone ever offers you an apple, run away! In The Real World, apples caused a lot of problems, so now they're seen as a very bad thing.

Chekhov's Gun

I'm not sure who this Chekhov guy was, but he was obviously a main character, because this is a really useful tool. Basically, anything that you as a character come across should have a purpose and reason to exist within the narrative, even if it seems really out of place at first.

EXAMPLE: That necklace I gave you before I was locked up by my evil vampire/dark angel/accountant family? You can bet your bottom adjective that it's a secret key to my room to help break me free.

Chandler's Law

Sometimes, when your plot stalls, your Author will invoke this. Basically, the worst case scenario for you suddenly happens.

Hope Spot

THE WORST. Are things going really well for you, dear soon-to-be main character? Look at your page number. If it's not in the triple digits, you're not near the end of the book, and this is a trap. It's designed to lull you into a false sense of security and happiness, before more terrible stuff happens.

Foreshadowing

Foreshadowing is a useful tool that predicts what is going to happen. But sometimes it's so subtle, readers don't even realize what it means until after the foreshadowed thing happens.

And sometimes, not so much.

EXAMPLE: You know how when you gaze into my eyes, it's as though you can see our life together? Yeah, that's foreshadowing. And it's about as subtle as that time your best friend shouted, "Don't date him, he's *clearly* a werelemur!"

Fridging

Hmm. Blondie suggested this one, but it's not in the dictionary. I'm going to ignore it.

A lesson on Fridging:
What is fridging? No, it's not when you open your fridge and stare at it, wondering what to eat. It's when the story has a really cool, dynamic character (almost always a woman, or someone of another marginalized background), and that character only exists to be put into dangerous or deadly situations to further the protagonist's (usually male character) journey.

Here's an example:

Character A is a smart, witty, brave woman, who is also the only diverse character in the whole book. She's dating her bland hero-dude, and suddenly, she's kidnapped! (More likely killed, but that example depresses me too much to write about.)

Bland hero-dude gets to angst about it for most of the book, go on his hero's journey, and probably even fall in love with someone new.

Character A? Yeah, she gets nothing. Even the Author forgets about her.

Motif

A repeating pattern which builds throughout the story.

Moral

An important lesson that the reader is hit on the head with throughout the story.

Red Herring

This is when you think something is going to be useful (like that guy you're dating at the start of the novel), and he turns out not to be (because you've met me). Or, if that doesn't make sense, here's another example. (Again! Me being generous! So generous! So wonderful! Certainly, never someone who would get deleted. Right?)

What if you and your friends uncover a mystery revolving around a very strange object—a goat—that appeared in your front yard. As you search, you unravel a mystery, dark and terrifying, full of intrigue . . .

And it has nothing to do with the goat.

That goat, my friend, was a red herring.

Not literally.

It's still a goat.

Not a fish.

Anyway.

Deus ex Machina

Ugh. Foreign languages. Um. This doesn't sound like a compliment or a curse word, which are my main two uses of any foreign language. Maybe it's . . . a spell? Yeah! That's it. It's a spell that summons some impossibly awesome ending, which the rest of the story has given no indication it should have.

Diabolus ex Machina

The bad version of the spell above. This one summons an antagonist greater than any you've ever faced, and makes the whole book even scarier, if a little more improbable.

Parent ex Machina

So, the previous two examples are all about a great and powerful force showing up at the end of the book and either solving or causing problems, right? Well. Nothing is more powerful or more scary than a parental figure who's finally remembered to act like an adult in a story. These characters can totally tie up the ending of a story in a neat bow.

Aries	**Chekhov's Gun**
Taurus	**Moral**
Gemini	**Plot Twists**
Cancer	**Passive-Aggressive Voice**
Leo	**Deus ex Machina**
Virgo	**Allusion**
Libra	**Dream Sequences**
Scorpio	**Hope Spot**
Sagittarius	**Chase Scene**
Capricorn	**Symbolism**
Aquarius	**Foil**
Pisces	**Flashbacks**

| l go-getter, you always have a plan, and know what you're going to do. |
| ble and practical, you never hesitate to give others advice, even if it's wrong. |
| ngeable and quirky, you can't be confined to a single plot. |
| ttle crabby and often moody, you can't help but let your nark show. Don't worry. This makes readers love you. |
| and bold, you charge into the endings of books and make stuff happen, regardless of logic. |
| ligent, focused, and committed, you've read more books n anyone else, so of course your story will refer to them. |
| e, kind, and romantic, you wish everything in life could be as dreamy as a, uh, dream. |
| erous, bold, and a little unpredictable, you live life according to no one else's rules. |
| Vibrant and exciting, you'll hunt down adventure wherever you can. |
| ermined, ambitious sort, you'll use every possible symbol ou can think of, until the book is almost unreadable. |
| Truthful and frank, you exist as a complete opposite to melodramatic characters. |
| lfless, kind, and nostalgic, you represent all the magic and wonder of the past. |

Parts of a Narrative

Now, let's dive into the story itself. All stories follow a pattern, which is almost identical to one perfect beat of my heart. Oddly enough, your heart also beats at the exact same rhythm as mine, because we all know heartbeats of those destined to be together match perfectly.

Below, I've included the map of plot, used by Authors for ever and ever and ever.

I think.

Anyway, you'll notice it starts at the beginning and ends at the end, just like it should.

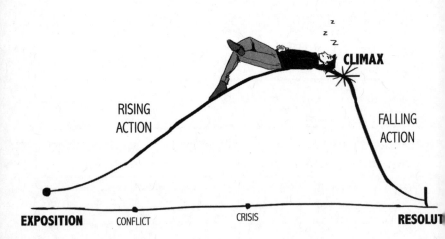

Exposition

This sets up the world of your story. Perhaps you gaze out your orphanage window up at the great castle where I live. Or you're walking into your first day of high school, where you catch a glimpse of me leaning attractively against a wall.

Conflict

The conflict is the primary battle—the thing driving that plot, examples of which we discussed earlier on page 148. It's me versus my evil ex. Or you, as the Chosen One, versus the evil overlord. Or me versus my feelings.

Stakes

This is what you, as a main character, risk losing when you engage in the story. If your story is about dating me when I am a dangerous, loner, rebel-type, you risk losing your friends, your good grades, and your free time. (You'll be spending all of it fixing my emotional issues.) On the other hand, in the same situation, my stakes are that I'll risk losing...uh... some spare time playing video games. Clearly, I am making a far greater sacrifice here. You're welcome.

Prologue

This is kind of like an opening chapter (see below), but with more flare. It might even be in an italic script to look extra fancy. This part of your story also follows no rules. It could be set thousands of years before your story opens or told from your mother's point of view. It might even rhyme. It also might not even need to exist, but your Author is too in love with it to remove it.

Opening Chapter

One morning, you wake up from a lovely dream (see "Dream Sequence, mentioned on page 262), climb out of bed, and stare into the mirror. After you describe yourself in great detail, as a good main character should, you go downstairs for breakfast. Here, plot will be conveyed to you. Perhaps it is breakfast time at an orphanage, where you will be told that you've reached the age where all orphans must go out into the world and seek their fortunes. Or maybe it's breakfast in your cozy, small town house, where your mother convinces you that the new school you'll be attending today will be wonderful. Or it could be the last breakfast you'll have with your family before the Great and Always Capitalized Event of Sorting occurs. This event will divide you from everyone you've known, as they will all be sorted into Boring-ish and you will be Unusual-ish.

Notice a theme here? Opening chapters start when something happens for the very first time. We call that the Inciting Incident, because alliteration is cool. Before I came along and suggested that, Authors just called it the Exciting Incident, which is just silly.

Rising Action

After that very first thing, events begin to build quickly. Things happen to you, or perhaps you happen to things (remember that whole lesson on agency?), in a manner that escalates every chapter.

There may be a montage where entire months fly by in a few paragraphs. Don't worry, that's completely normal. And, no, somehow none of us will need haircuts after.

Climax

This is it. The most epic moment of all. In this part of the story, you will achieve true main character status as you face down whatever bad things are about to happen. Every moment has led to this one.

Let's just hope you don't faint and let someone else save the day. (But if you do, please know that I'll be brooding somewhere nearby and ready to swoop in.)

Resolution

All those loose ends (except for those necessary for a sequel) will be wrapped up neatly. Relationships will be defined, best friends will reappear from the misty fog all supporting characters fade into . . . This is also where any lies you've told your love interest should probably be revealed, along with any other items on your to-do list that weren't "save the world."

The Ending

The last moments. Make sure they're good ones. Perhaps you should kiss or promise your undying love or just smirk winningly.

Epilogue

Surprise! That wasn't actually the ending at all. This gives you one more happy/cute moment. There are usually babies involved. Or, if this is a contemporary novel, a scene taking place on your college campus where you are cheerily setting out on the rest of your life.

Theme

Your reader will realize your story was actually about this after they've set down your book and walked away from it—what it means to belong or that beauty is what's on the inside or that having a lot of money can make life much easier.

Revision

Ever felt like your story stinks? What if you're wandering around on some quest and nothing makes sense?

Don't worry! Your Author is probably just revising. It's a little-known fact that Authors don't actually receive their books from a secret mountain cavern full of lovely, solid gold stories and guarded by a dragon. Instead, they must actually . . . create them. This process is not at all like falling in love, which we know is instantaneous after one very long moment of eye contact. Instead, Authors must write, rewrite, and edit their stories until they are ready to be read.

The process of revision is a bumpy one for fictional characters to endure. Sometimes you'll be in the middle of a scene, and then your Author doesn't know how to finish it, so they'll simply skip the scene's ending, and move to the next. They may even forget to come back.

While you're waiting for your Author to perfect her prose, I suggest taking up a hobby. Me? I knit my eyebrows together. I've produced many lovely scarves this way.

After revisions, your Author will send her story to friends, which is when you begin your most important task of all as a main character . . . Making sure people never forget you.

NARRATIVE INTERLUDE: WHILE OUR BRILLIANT HERO BROODS, EVIL TAKES THE STAGE

Blondie growled in frustration, then quickly checked herself in the mirror to ensure she hadn't become a werewolf. What else could she do to get through to Broody? She'd even sent the supernatural beings in to try and change ridiculous Broody's brain. It hadn't worked. He was so certain that he was right—that his way of telling a story was the only right one.

And that wasn't fair.

It wasn't fair to her or to Broody's best friend or to the countless other supporting characters who deserved to have their stories told, too.

To say nothing of how unfair it was for all the real-life teens who never got a chance to see themselves reflected as main characters on the page or screen. Surely it was worth trying one more time for their sakes.

Granted, Blondie had to admit to herself one of the reasons she cared about those kids was she . . . she wanted to be seen as a hero, too. She wanted the fan art and squeeing and all the wonderful excitement Broody brought out in people.

She also figured admitting to herself that she wasn't 100 percent magnanimous was a pretty good way to ensure she wasn't the actual villain of the story.

Blondie hurried out of the great hall near Broody's room. Already, the dystopian setting had vanished, replaced by a sort of medieval fantasy village, complete with roaming unicorns. (Which seemed pretty darn magical until you remembered their poop was full of glitter and a pain to get off the bottom of your shoes.) But Blondie was glad the setting had changed. It would be easier to find who she needed to speak with.

The wise mentor character lived in a small teahouse with her wife, down the street from other various helpful characters and magical beings. Blondie snuck trips to see them from time to time, though, as an antagonist, she knew she should stick to the evil side of town.

But it was just so . . . dramatic over there. All that cape twirling and evil laugh practicing. No, she'd much rather be among the helpful characters. After all, she was trying to help Broody. Just in a rather . . . villainous way.

Some traits were just at the core of a character's nature.

The mentor opened the door, her graying hair twisted into a braid, wearing a genre-incongruous sweatshirt. Blondie supposed if you tutored enough heroes, you got to wear whatever you wanted. Behind her, a fire flickered, and the scent of home-made brownies—truly the most magical scent in the world—wafted toward her.

"Blondie! Come in, come in. Sit. Have tea. What can I help you with? How is your quest?"

A quest. It thrilled Blondie to even hear those words. She knew she didn't deserve a quest. Villains had motives, yes, and goals, but quests were for good people—for heroes. But here, in this little cottage, with her friends, she could enjoy the words. The mentor had known about Blondie's work for weeks. "It's . . . it's frustrating," she admitted, sipping her tea. "I feel like I can never quite get Broody to understand what it's like . . . to not be a main character."

"Hmmm." The mentor pondered this pensively and with a great deal of thought, as befits a wise mentor. "Perhaps you should show him the work fans have done to try and correct some of these issues?"

"Oh? I'm sorry, Wise Mentor, but I don't know what you're talking about."

"Why, the Fandom, my dear!" The Mentor clapped her hands, rings sparkling in the sunlight. Legend held that she had once been a great and wonderful teen protagonist, experiencing many adventures. Blondie had no doubt it was true.

"What is the Fandom?"

"Oh, Broody will tell you all about it if you ask him, I'm sure. In short, it is the place where we supporting characters are often given more time and attention. Fan art is drawn, fic is written. The Fandom is truly a magical place."

"More magical than this fantasy setting we're currently in?" Blondie skeptically raised her eyebrow in a doubting, dubious manner.

"Absolutely," the Mentor said. A powerful character with a strong internal narrative, she needed no extra adverbs to convey intent. "Nothing possesses greater magic than the mind of a creative individual."

After tea, brownies, and a little chitchat, Blondie resolved to go back to Broody and force him to tell her more about this strange and wonderful place known as the Fandom.

She found the intrepid wannabe Author doing the thing all writers do best . . . procrastinating.

Broody let a paper airplane soar at her. It missed, crashing into the wall, where many of its brave, barely flight-worthy brethren had already met their ends. "Yo, Blondie."

She shook her head before bending down to pick up a crumpled plane. With a few crisp folds, she resurrected its wings and sent it back to Broody.

It flew perfectly.

She was quite good at engineering, although usually all she got to engineer in a book was drama.

"Tell me about fanfic?" she asked, again leaning against the wall, while he marveled at her paper airplane.

"You don't know about fanfic?"

"No, Broody, that's why I asked."

He mumbled, and then said, "Well, sometimes characters ask you about stuff they already know just 'cause the reader doesn't know it."

One of her perfectly manicured brows shot up. "Really. Me? Caring about readers. Are you out of your mind?"

"Hah." he rubbed the back of his neck. "Good point."

Once she left, Broody had to wait until the genre shifted back to contemporary, and his note-book changed into a laptop. Then he searched the Internet for the word "fan fiction."

After he spit out his hazelnut-cinnamon-mocha-soy-latte on his screen in shock, he regained composure (as well as a new laptop) and started to write.

It has come to my attention that some people think one's journey is over once they become a main character.

Not so!

Read on and find out more.

CHAPTER 8

YOU'RE A MAIN CHARACTER . . . NOW WHAT?

You've done it! You've picked your story, you've found a great plot, and you've won true love. The bad guys are conquered. The supporting characters have supported you while having absolutely no identifiable personalities of their own. Everything is as it should be. Now what? Do you think your story's over? Oh, dear, sweet, clueless readers . . . The world is an open book for main characters!

Literally.

But also figuratively.

I probably didn't use either of those words correctly, but I don't care. I'm too good-looking to worry about things like proper usage.

In fact, thanks to my chiseled abs, piercing gaze, and gravel-softening voice, readers will never get tired of me. (Even if the words used to describe me sound more like power tools than any human attributes.) They'll love me, no matter if I reappear in a sequel, on a TV show, or even lend my best bits of dialogue to delicious scented candles, guaranteed to smell almost exactly like my personal combination of lavender, sandalwood, soap, pine trees, and *man*. Readers *love* candles almost as much as they love books, though not as much as they love me.

I'll give you a couple of minutes to go light some candles and retousle your hair before we jump into life as a main character after your first book.

Sequels

You know all those plots we talked about? Saving the kingdom/prom/puppy? They are now over—but do not fear, my friend. A lot of them have set you up for a sequel, which is really nifty. Unless your book never gets a sequel and you're caught in a cliffhanger ending forever and ever. Not that that's ever happened to me. I successfully scale down from all cliffhangers, and go straight into my readers' hearts.

Sequels are books that follow your first book appearance detailing more of your adventures and, more importantly, your beauty, and give you even more awesome one-liners. There will be more romantic moments that might seem highly problematic if one thinks about them too hard, more plot twists, and more kissing. There should *always* be more kissing in the sequel.

Does this sound like a lot of work? Tough luck. Your Author has probably plotted about eighteen thousand sequels, so you better stock up on Gatorade and protein, 'cause you've got a long journey ahead of you. You might be in sequels for years to come. I've got buddies who are still trapped in sequels being written *after* their Authors died.

Authors love sequels. That's why they have all those little asides and hints about bigger stories in their first book. You know that supporting character who said the one vague thing about your older brother in Book One?

Oh yeah, that's gonna make a comeback in Book Two. Or Book Ten. Who knows?

But what if your book tied everything up in a neat bow?

Never doubt an Author's ability to pull a plot twist out of thin air. Thin air, of course, being shorthand for the Author's preferred drink/snack/music/procrastination combo. (Seriously, do Authors ever work? Anytime I peer out of this glowing three-dimensional box she's trapped me inside—which is fascinating, when one considers that I am merely a two-dimensional character—my Author is always snacking, browsing Pinterest, or researching obscure name meanings.)

Once your Author is haunted by the terrifying Ghost of Deadlines Future, she'll start to throw random words on the page. She'll frantically mash keys until a story begins to take shape, which will, of course, star you and any other main characters she can quickly grab.

Authors get frantic when the Deadline Ghost shows up. I'm not sure why. He announces his arrival pretty obviously with a big red X on the calendar and all. And still, they complain he came out of nowhere. . . .

Anyway, the more frantic your Author is, the stranger the plot twists you'll be put through.

Don't believe me? You really should. You wouldn't believe all the things I've suffered in sequels. I've had amnesia, been kidnapped, learned I had an older, more evil, even broodier brother. I've been brainwashed and turned into a werelemur. Don't worry, I handled it all with my usual, incomparable poise, and have never shed more than one single tear per sequel.

Speaking of amnesia, let me warn you about a very dangerous disease affecting some main characters in sequels. It's called "Character Development Dysfunction," or CDD for short. This disease primarily affects male love interests, although it can happen to villains-turned-good-guys, parental figures, figures of authority, or even main female characters. Sadly, I, too, have suffered this condition, and it breaks my heart every time. Or it would, if I had any heart left to break. All I have are some shattered shards that glitter in my cold, cold eyes.

What is CDD? It's when all the character development you've undergone in the first book simply . . . vanishes in the second. No, it's not amnesia or mind-wiping. Those have the same end result to be sure, but they have clear plot-centered explanations. CDD is like the Author wiped everyone's minds with absolutely no explanation.

Still don't understand? Let's try an example. In the first book, I learned how to trust my love interest after spending centuries as a cold, dangerous monster known as the Tooth Fairy. Through the power of love—and really good dental hygiene—my sugary-sweet heroine taught me it's okay to trust people, and convinced me to stop stealing their teeth as they slept.

But in the second book, I'm back to being a dangerous, renegade fairy, prying molars out of people's mouths. There's no reason for my backslide into antagonist-mode, no plot-related events that caused my regression. The Author simply realized that when I became a reformed Tooth Fairy, there was no plot left for her to work with.

If CDD happens to you, be brave.

Other than CDD, sequels can be a lot of fun. You get even more chances to show off, to save your love interest, to save the day, to save the reader from boredom. General A+ hero stuff, really.

Sometimes, you might even become a POV character, even if you weren't one in the first book. Or—this is even more exciting—the sequel might be written *entirely* from your POV. That's a huge win! Just think of how much more brooding you'll be able to do when your reader can hear all of your brilliant, emotional thoughts!

But as great as sequels can be, there are a few other things I must warn you about. It's not always smooth sailing. Sometimes strange plot twists might even . . . write you out of the story. Terrifying, I know. But, as main characters, we can persevere. I'll even share my tips for ensuring you remain a main character.

The Scary Part of Sequels

A Rival Love Interest Shows Up

This is so frustrating. After going through all the hard work of successfully capturing the heart of your one true love, she goes off and starts swooning in someone else's arms. Totally unfair!

Who is this upstart? Not to make you paranoid, but it could be anyone—your older sibling, or a new person visiting your town, or your love interest's childhood best friend/mentor/daydream reappearing as an actual character intent on wooing her.

You'll have to up all your swoonworthy moments and your attractiveness (remember: $a^2 + b^2$) in order to triumph against this challenger.

But Broody! you cry, tears like perfect sapphires shining in your eyes. *How on earth can I prove that I am the best love interest ever? What if this guy has even more adjectives than I do?*

First of all, stop moping. No Broody has ever won his protagonist back by moping. I mean, a few chapters of a mope can give you lovely moments of staring up into the sky, stars glittering almost as brightly as the tears swimming in your aquamarine eyes but, eventually, you've got to do something to win your love interest back. Try saving the day or haunting her dreams so she remembers how wonderful you are. Those have often worked for me.

Or just show up and stare very intensely at her. Unyielding eye contact with no blinking is always sexy. And not creepy at all.

You Get Killed Off
Ouch. Yeah. This one hurts. Even if it's in a beautifully tragic moment where you sacrifice yourself to save not only your love interest, but a kitten, a group of innocent children, and the plot, nothing changes the fact that you're . . . uh . . . dead. It's *really* hard to be a main character after you're dead.

The best you can do is hope that your death occurred in a dream sequence and you'll thankfully and miraculously be alive in the next chapter.

Or maybe you'll come back as a sexy, undead hero. Think vampire, or cute zombie, or a ghost with really great hair.

If that fails, cross all your fingers that you'll get a prequel. I'll discuss that more on page 299.

You Find Out You're a Jerk

So, you ended Book One on a good note, right? You saved the day, people like you, you like yourself.

But do you, really?

In truth, all of your feelings were a ruse. In this type of sequel, the reader will learn (and heck, it might be news to you, too) that every nice thing you ever did was only part of a long, elaborate trap meant to ensnare your love interest. Maybe you're working for a bad guy even bigger and badder than the antagonist of the first book. Maybe you have a secret grudge against the main character's family. Maybe your Author totally had no idea what to write and making you secretly evil was way easier than trying to remember that she actually had developed your personality already.

Your Sequel is Written by a Different Author

I probably shouldn't even mention this very scary possibility, but it is my sworn duty to provide you with a guide to all things a main character might encounter, and I would be failing in my obligations to you if I did not at least attempt to explain this phenomenon.

It's confusing to wake up in a book and realize that the words being written and the dialogue being placed in your roguishly beautiful mouth have not been crafted by the same Author as the first book.

Let's stop biting our lips until they bleed and let out those breaths we didn't know we were holding. We can handle this!

Just trust the new Author to also fall madly in love with you, and that she'll craft you another beautiful story.

You Have a New Love Interest

This might seem strange. Didn't you spend all that time working to get your chocolate-haired, blueberry-eyed, vanilla-scented ~~pancake~~ love interest to notice you in the last book?

Luckily, female characters are entirely interchangeable!

This is more common in movies, which we'll be covering a bit later, but this possibility can happen in books, too, especially if they're in your POV.

You might be a detective, or a spy, or a superhero, or a dog walker. You know, a job that takes up a lot of your spare time and also involves risking your life a lot. That's probably the reason you have totally forgotten about your last love interest, as well. Totally understandable.

Your Sequel Takes So Long to Come Out, Everyone Forgets Who You Are

Okay, so you won't even notice this from inside your story, but let's be honest. Every main character secretly breaks the fourth wall sometimes, to peer out into the reader's real world and see how things are going. Obviously, we hope your sequel comes out at the perfect moment. Long enough after Book One that readers are eagerly awaiting it, planning to skip school/work/sleep in order to read it the moment they get the book in their hands, and soon enough, that they still remember all those random facts about your backstory.

But what if your Author has trouble writing the sequel, or it gets delayed? It's possible that by the time readers have it in their hands, they might move you to the bottom of their To-Be-Read pile. Or, worse, they might decide they've "outgrown you."

Ouch.

Not to worry! I firmly believe that if you follow all the steps in this book, you'll lock in a main character identity so strongly, readers will never be able to forget you.

###

So, there we have it. Common issues with sequels, and how to survive them. But maybe your Author really, really doesn't want to write a sequel. Does that mean your days as a main character are over?

Uh, am I a thoughtful, considerate, and respectful boyfriend?

(The answer to both questions is no, FYI.)

Maybe your future is not a sequel. Maybe it's a book set in the same universe. Those can be okay. Granted, there's a risk that you'll be reduced to a supporting character.

Well, *you* might. I never would be. I'm far too magnificent to ever be a supporting character.

What are these non-sequel-and-yet-connected books of which I speak? There are a few types, and I've made sure to detail all of them below. Because let me tell you, as a man, I greatly enjoy explaining things.

Prequels

These are the books that come *before* your story starts. They might detail your childhood, your first kiss, your every waking thought until the day you waltz into the main story.

Or, you know, any other story that occurs before the main story. But I personally think *my* life before the book starts is the most interesting, you know? So, perhaps we skip learning anything else about you and give me a prequel story.

Companion Novels

You know how there's that one best friend of yours in your book who *almost* seems good enough to be a main character? Or that guy friend of mine who's totally almost as swoonworthy as me?

Surprise! They get to be the star of their own novel.

Yes, unfortunately, it is possible that someone other than me gets to star in a novel. And it's very, very annoying. But my Author promises if I don't grumble too much, I'll still get to have a cameo. I'll appear in the background, smirking happily as my love interest ruffles my hair. Even better, I might appear in multiple scenes, acting as a mentor to the new main character. Then, I'll be able to help him navigate the plot with my brilliant words of wisdom. My advice is, after all, golden, as you've probably realized by reading through this wonderful masterpiece of mine.

And we all know my readers will desperately flip through the whole book looking for that tiny scene of mine. That's the only reason they'll bother buying the book, of course.

The Next Generation

In some stories, you and your love interest get married. You know what comes next?

Babies.

No, Broody. You just . . . UGH. Reader, I'm sorry for his general cluelessness. We both know that's not . . . Never mind. I can't even begin to explain how wrong he is right here.

xoxo, B

That's right. You and your love interest will have some babies. Don't worry. They'll be adorable. There will probably be at least one scene describing how amazing a parent you are, even if you've shown absolutely no interest in kids before.

But, my friend, no one actually wants to read about babies, because they have even less control over their emotions than I do, so your Author will skip a huge chunk of time, and suddenly, the babies will be *teenagers*.

It is a well-known fact that the only beings louder, cuter, wilder, and with less impulse control than toddlers are teenagers. Also, teenagers can speak whole sentences, drive cars, and save the world way better than toddlers can.

As for you? Are you worried that by the time your children are old enough to drive, you might be showing signs of age? Don't worry, you'll still be attractive. If you're a woman, you'll have a few small creases around the corners of your eyes. If you're a man, you'll have a few strands of silver fetchingly highlighting your dark hair. Otherwise, you'll look and act just like you did as a teenager. Isn't that great?

Even stranger, your children will look almost identical to either you or your love interest. The boy child may have the perfect blend of your gemstone eyes and your love interest's button nose. Or, perhaps, the girl child will look like you, the father, for really boring symbolism or something.

Regardless, these children will also be main characters. This is because, once achieved, main character status *is* hereditary. All children of main characters inherit their parents' power to control plot. In fact, they might even have a love interest that is the child of the unlucky love interest in your own book.

The Far Future/Reincarnation

Perhaps your Author doesn't want to picture you as an aging adult, or perhaps she hates babies. Another way to have a spin-off novel: your Author ventures into a distant future of the world she introduced in your book. Your name and your love story will be known as a legend to a new generation of main characters.

These protagonists might even be reincarnations of the beings you were in your own story. So it's like getting to experience your story all over again, but in different outfits.

Now that we've talked about babies, let's discuss what to name the tiny bundles of main character joy, as well as what their role in a story will be. Here's a quick way to learn your future, and I guarantee it's 141 percent less frustrating than getting a half-complete prophecy.

Not that I would know anything about that . . .

Choose your favorite color.
1.   Red
2.   Green
3.   Silver
4.   I like them all equally!
5.   Pink
6.   Blue
7.   Black

If you chose **1**, your child's first name will be **Gerald** (but he'll go by "Danger").

If you chose **2**, your child's first name will be **Maximillian** (but he'll go by Max).

If you chose **3**, your child's first name will be **Arvenia**.

If you chose **4**, your child's first name will be **Tulip**.

If you chose **5**, your child's first name will be **Melinda Rosa Nicola**.

If you chose **6**, your child's first name will be **Bob**.

If you chose **7**, your child's first name will be **Jet**.

Choose your favorite way to defeat an antagonist.
  A. With a weapon, duh!
  B. Sarcasm with a dash of snark
  C. True love
  D. I prefer to wait for their own evil plan to stop them
  E. Uh, does "become one" count?

If you chose **A**, your child will be **a strong warrior, destined to train the next chosen one**.

If you chose **B**, your child be **a delicate flower of a princess/prince and will probably be kidnapped within a week after their first birthday**.

If you chose **C**, your child will **grow up to be the greatest villain your land has ever known**.

If you chose **D**, your child will be **the bookish type (a scholar if you're in a fantasy world, a valedictorian otherwise) and their story will be all about them learning to have fun**.

If you chose **E**, your child will be . . . **the most magnificent of all. Your child will become a mini-Broody, following exactly in my footsteps**.

We've covered all the various types of book-related spin-offs that await you in your future, but perhaps you're wondering if your destiny might hold something a bit less . . . literary. Maybe you're getting a little tired of chasing after adjectives. And paper cuts. Ugh!

Don't worry. There are many more options available to you. Your future is as limitless as the number of shades of gemstone hues my eyes could be.

Movie Deals!

So, your book has done well, and Hollywood has come calling. They've heard just what an incredible main character you are. You preen and pose for them, and *bam!* You've got a movie deal.

I used to think a movie deal was as good as it gets. A chance to shine, to have my beautiful face shown to the entire world on a massive screen. What more could I want?

Uh, to have the directors actually read my beautiful book. That would be a fantastic start.

Here's the thing about movies. There is no guarantee they'll even come close to following your book's story. They may totally ignore plot lines, change dialogue, and they will absolutely cut out at least one crucial character. A movie can be so different from the book, you barely even feel like yourself. Sometimes, they'll never even make a movie of your sequel, and then movie-you will always be left wondering what happens next.

But sometimes, the movie does truly capture your magnificence, and that's really what you should hope for.

Plus, movies come with all sorts of cool bonus opportunities like theme songs! And merchandise! As long as you don't mind having one actor/actress become known as you, your face will be plastered everywhere.

QUICK TIP: always attempt to have your trilogy of books turned into four movies for maximum main character moment mastery.

TV Show

TVs are like movie screens, except smaller. In case you didn't know.

Here's the weird thing about TV shows. They can end suddenly or go on longer than that time you had to watch your love interest dance with someone else at prom. And just like in a movie, you might as well say goodbye to the idea that your book holds all the truth you'll ever need in your story. Since TV shows can stretch out for season after season, they'll have to invent new things, so just cross your fingers and hope they're good inventions.

TV shows also have a lot of their own devices and techniques. For example, there's something called a "musical episode" where, for whatever reason, every character in the show will sing. And if you thought my voice was a thunderously lovely thing to listen to before, just wait until you hear me belt out a romantic show tune.

Also, every teenage character will be played by twenty-something actors, but that's okay. No one will notice.

These are, of course, just two options, but truly, your possibilities as a main character may be limitless. Living the main character lifestyle means your story can transcend all types of entertainment and art. Way back in the day, my ancestor, Broodington Hottietrousers, frequently worked with the great Author, Billy Shakespeare. The Author gave Broodington awesome roles like being a prince of Denmark or an overly dramatic young man in love. Do you think Broodington realized his stories would inspire ballets, paintings, and musicals with gang members who snap their fingers in menacing unison? Absolutely not!

I mean, I know you'll never be anywhere close to as magnificent as I am, but let me tell you about the myriad of media in which I've appeared.

Hi Reader:

Broody, as always, is being an over-simplifying dork. If you find yourself the main character of one of these stories, relish it!

Perhaps someday you'll be the one giving advice to other characters in this form of media.

xoxo, B

Comic Books

These are illustrated stories. They're very cool, even if they're rather confusing because they include tons of alternate timelines, identity switching, and universes that explode. Sometimes. Other times they can be dark and gritty or slice of life or . . . Yeah, I guess they're just like books . . . made of comic strips. Wow.

Just try not to worry too much, and enjoy when cool call-out bubbles like BAM! appear when you punch someone.

Manga

Also illustrated stories and equally cool. These come from Japan and have a distinctive beautiful style. (Especially when I'm a character in them. Then I'm even more beautiful than any other character.) It's worth noting that my Brooding Awesomeness can exist in stories across the world, and each culture will give me their own unique set of tropes.

Sometimes, I think about how nice it must be to be Broody, and simplify the world's different cultures as all revolving around him. Am I right, reader, or am I right?

xoxo, B

Graphic Novels

Illustrated stories that are much longer and sometimes more pretentious. They might not have sound effect bubbles, which is a bummer, but they're very likely to win awards. Those are almost as good.

Video Games

These are like movies that the player gets to control. Wow! That means if you fail in your story, it's not your fault or the writer's fault. It's whoever is playing your game and constantly failing at beating a boss/collecting enough widgets/tapping a button fast enough.

I knew I would like video games when I found out one of the earliest ones involved saving a princess from a castle. That's one of my all-time-favorite hobbies!

P.S. You know who never gets saved from castles? Evil ex-girlfriends.

Board Games

Like a video game, except there are small pieces you can lose if you aren't careful. Do not lose the Broody game piece. Do not pass GO. Do not collect $200.

Merchandise

Remember how I mentioned candles? If you're a lucky main character, your witty words will be on everything from mugs to tote bags. That's reason 1,417 to have quippy one-liners prepared at all times, and to deploy them as often as you can in your story. Even when you're running for your life.

Actually, make that *especially* when you're running for your life.

###

Fandom

Now that we've talked about all the money-making ventures you could star in, I'd like to take some time to talk about a subject near and dear to my heart: myself.

Well, no.

I mean, I'll always talk about myself, but I wanted to specifically talk about the group of people who love to put their creative powers to use talking about me.

I want to talk about the Fandom.

This word is a combination of two words: *Fanatic* and *Kingdom*.

It's a kingdom full of people fanatical about you, and you are their king and ruler. It's a pretty sweet gig if you can get it.

And how do you get to have your own fan kingdom? Well, if you follow all my other advice and become a handsome, dynamic, witty main character,

then you, too, might be lucky enough to be given this rare and precious gift.

Some common aspects in the world of fandom may be a little confusing to an outsider: namely, when the fandom ignores fact. You see, the work you hail from will be known as *canon*. However, sometimes your fans find the canon a little boring. Maybe your Author didn't include enough kissing or made your world about as diverse as a loaf of white bread. In these cases, the fans will step in, prepared to add their own unique twists on your world. Here are some handy terms, so you'll be prepared:

Fanon

This is when your fans decide collectively on something that might not actually appear in the text. For example, there is a very nice tower in your castle. This tower is only mentioned once in passing, but your fans have decided that all young couples in your castle scurry off to the tower to make out. As the years pass by, and more fandom works depict this tower as the Tower of Loooove, it grows so commonplace, many forget it was never in your book in the first place.

Head Canon

This is like fanon, but for a smaller group of people, perhaps even just one person. My fan, Patrick, is quite sure my favorite drink to order at a coffee shop is a Double Syrup Peppermint White Chocolate Mocha. Patrick will argue with anyone who tries to tell him that I would rather drink black coffee.

(Don't tell anyone, but Patrick is right.)

Speaking of being right, here's the thing: I, Broody McHottiepants, always think the fans are right. No matter what their head canon tells them, I will respect their choices. Fans love the works, and love me and other characters enough to dedicate their time to making more art about us. Therefore, they should be given the utmost respect.

Even if they give me silly nicknames like "Broodster Cuddlepants."

One other thing to note. Sometimes, in fandom . . . I appear when I wasn't originally in the work. How could this miracle happen? Simple. A fan creator takes a character that is far, far beneath me in the original work, and morphs him into a version of me. I consider this the greatest honor, especially if they also give me leather pants.

Fan Fiction

This is probably the easiest for you, as a written fictional character, to understand. Fan fiction is fiction that has been written by fans. (Really, it must be exhausting being such a clueless main character. Good thing I'm here to explain everything to you.) These are stories, so they may very well use some of those same narrative tools I mentioned earlier. However, there's much more freedom in fan fiction. Authors can do things like . . . skip the concept of "plot" entirely. Or they can break the fourth wall and have the characters directly talk to them! (A character, talking to Authors. How strange and novel a concept.)

Fanfic is its own beautiful world, full of its own terminology. Every main character should consider exploring its realms, at least for a little while. Just watch out for OOC (Out of Character) moments, those moments where you find yourself acting completely unlike yourself.

Also, beware unfinished fics—stories that have not been updated in years, leaving you perpetually in plot limbo.

Here are some of my favorite places to stay in Fanfic Land:

The Beach of Drabbles

Here is a very pleasant place to pass your days. Drabbles are short snippets of lovely prose, sometimes inspired by a word, such as "teatime" or "raindrop" or "defenestration."

Yes, I'd definitely like to write a Broody drabble about defenestration . . .

Cafe One Shot

One shots are great for a quick visit. They're a self-contained work of indeterminable length, and are always enjoyable to star in, since you don't have to work as hard to keep things like plot going. Sometimes you can just lay in bed the whole story. So relaxing.

AU (Alternate Universe) Village

Ah yes, this village can be quite confusing on your first visit. In short, AUs are stories where the characters from your book exist, but in completely different settings and situations. One time, I was a handsome young starship captain in a thrilling sci-fi adventure, but when I visited AU Village, I was suddenly a high school sophomore in a band. Sometimes, these stories are so different I can barely recognize myself. And sometimes, they are just characters playing dress-up.

Crossover County

An interesting place to visit, although I think I might develop a slight inferiority complex if I lived there. In these stories, the fan Author combines your story with another one, and lets the sparks fly.

Let's say the fan Author loves your book and also loves that movie about wizards in space. She decides to put you into the space setting, allowing you to influence and change that story's plot.

Sometimes, you'll even get to kiss a love interest from a different story. How cool is that?

Fluff Factory

Ah, fluff. My happy place. These fics are dedicated to feel-good feelings, which are the very best type of feelings. Adjectives and swoonworthy moments abound. There's no need for plot in these stories, which merely set up a cute moment, and let you revel in the feels, like sinking into a bed made of cotton candy. Oftentimes, these are romantic in nature, and give a character like me a chance to woo someone I might not in the actual story. For example, Blon—No. Broody. Get ahold of yourself, man! Maybe do some push-ups, or eyebrow raises. Stop thinking that.

Self-Insert Shop

This is a place where the writer of the fic drops themselves into the fictional world. They might be self-aware, meaning they know the plot and are actively trying to change it. (This is a very useful power when you mistakenly were killed off in the original book. Because, obviously, any time you were killed off was a giant, glaring mistake.) Other times, fans pay little attention to the rules of your fictional world, running rampant through it, changing things on their own whims like power-mad demigods.

There's also . . . *racy* fanfic, but there's no need to discuss those. We've clearly established already that I prefer to keep my activities to "rolling around on a bed made of metaphors."

Needless to say, fanfic is full of many more types of stories, and I encourage you to explore them all. Part of the fun of being a main character is getting to be in even more stories, right?

Yes, yes, so lovely to be a main character, and be in even more stories than one already has on a shelf. Thanks, Broody. Rub it in.

I wonder if Broody even realizes how much we supporting characters live for the day we have one piece of fan art, one fan fiction story? How little we have, and how much we hope for?

Nah. He's probably too busy writing himself fan fiction about him falling in love with his reflection. Even if I thought there were a few moments, just a few, where he might have . . .

No, I'm being ridiculous. Let me just talk about fanfic for a moment instead.

When there are no stories that reflect your character, when you have nothing but a shallow, poorly depicted version of yourself on the pages of a book, you end up living for fan fiction. At least there, you've got a chance you might see yourself in the narrative.

Could I ever make Broody see that? How lucky he is to be . . . who he is?

Ugh. I'm turning into a sap. I have got to stop hanging around Broody. His love of melodrama is contagious.

xoxo, Blondie

Fan Art

This, my friend, is one of my favorite things in the whole, entire world. People drawing pictures of *me*!

Or, uh, other main characters.

But really, *me*! We haven't talked a lot about me recently.

Talented artists use their magical powers to capture my beautiful face, and then share it with the world. I really enjoy fan art, and not just because it's a chance for me to stare deeply into my own sparkling gemstone eyes. It's fun because everyone sees my beauty and captures it in their own style, so it's almost like the artists of the world are making a Broody-filled army.

Cosplay

Speaking of flattery, I do love seeing fans dress up as me. This is called cosplay, and is a unique way of taking my two-dimensional beauty and recreating it "in real life," or "IRL" as all the hip kids say. Cosplay costumes can be so casual, one would be able to attend a real coffee shop in them, or so complex they won't fit through a doorway.

Your Author has put a lot of time into describing your outfits (hopefully) and, therefore, these cosplay creations can be really fun to see. If you truly

represent an iconic sense of fashion in your work,
be prepared for people to dress like you for years
to come. Why, I once tossed on a black vest over
my white shirt and navy trousers, with a blaster in
a holster at my side . . . and people still sport that
fashion, decades later. That's icon status right there.

Dear Broody,
   I am a big fan of yours.
Do you ever think it's strange,
though, how sometimes your
fandom tries so hard to make
your world more diverse, give
supporting characters more
stage time, sometimes even
changing the relationships in
your books? Do you think it's
because these fans are reacting
to a need they may have to see
themselves on the page? What
do you have to say about that?
                    —A huge fan
        who is obviously not your ex

Hmm. How odd to get fan mail before my book is even entirely written! Ah, well, I have included it here, within the pages of this lovely work for posterity.

Dearest fan, when you buy this book, you'll be able to read my answer.

And that is.

Uh . . .

I don't know? I . . . I never thought of fandom as being used for that purpose. I mainly just log on and search the Internet for beautiful new drawings of me.

Still, I suppose, fan, perhaps you could be a little right. It's possible that sometimes these fan writers, just like fiction Authors, are writing things into the world they wish would happen or wish to understand.

So, I suppose I am glad they can do that. And if it involves me being extra swoonworthy? Why, all the better!

Hopefully this chapter has shown you that there's so much more to a main character's life than just that very first book. Even if you never reach a sequel, you might find true happiness in fanfic or in a comic book adaptation. Sometimes, books never receive the attention they deserve, which is a very sad thing, but the squeeing of even one fan is enough to help heal a protagonist's heart.

Truly, fans are among the most magical of all beings.

Oh, and if you want to draw some fan art of me? Just give me a call and I'll happily pose for you anytime.

IS IT STILL AN INTERLUDE IF THERE'S NOTHING AFTER?

"That's how you're going to end it?" Blondie asked Broody in disbelief.

He blinked, baffled and full of bafflement. She'd read the book?

He at least was not surprised that Blondie was in the room, since she'd been around a lot, bringing him coffee and helpful books on writing. Sometimes, she even volunteered to look things up in a magical book called the dictionary.

She said there was a thesaurus, too, but that he would be certain to abuse its mystical powers, so he wasn't allowed to have that one anywhere near him.

Broody had been amazed by how helpful, how interesting . . . how fun Blondie had been.

Had being the key word since, right now, she was glaring furiously, intensely, ragingly.

Broody wasn't even sure if that last one was a real word, but even if it wasn't, it deserved real word status.

And then, Blondie threw his just-finished book at his head.

He caught it with the cat-like reflexes of a cat (or a werelemur, but who could tell the difference) and tilted his head. "I . . . What are you doing in my room?"

"I read your whole book!"

"Oh! Awesome. Great. Did you . . . like it?" He paused, trying to remember what else Authors said in these situations. Now that he was, officially, an Author, he wanted to sound professional. "If you did, you should, uh, give it a five star review!"

She rolled her eyes. "No! I didn't like it."

"Why not?" He'd heard not everyone would be a fan of an Author's work, so he was prepared for constructive criticism, as long as it was delivered in sandwich form, between two compliments. Or with an actual sandwich.

"Because it didn't help me at all!" Her bright eyes flashed dangerously.

Broody took a step back. He wasn't retreating, no. Broody was far too manly to retreat, ever. "Help you do what?"

"Become a main character, of course!" Blondie threw herself on the bed in her best impersonation of a main character's dramatic sort of action. Of course, she wasn't one, and the action only succeeded in getting her hair stuck to her lip gloss.

Broody cautiously walked closer, and with great attention, in a tentative manner, sat by her side. "Blondie . . . is that why you asked me to write this book? Is that why you challenged me?"

She nodded miserably.

It was all starting to make sense to him. All the questions she had asked. The trips they'd taken together over the last 325 pages. Heck, even the ghosts who had haunted him. Blondie had been pushing him to think outside of his main character bubble, to change.

And he hadn't.

But in that moment, he finally understood. Seeing a character who'd never been a hero, who could never become a hero, even though she'd read his book, cry made something shift in the very depths of his soul.

He put his hand, shyly, nervously, in a manner not at all befitting a Broody, on her shoulder. "Blondie?" It was a question, soft and gentle, that would make more sense coming from a supporting character. Not from him. He wasn't supposed to communicate.

Or care.

She slowly lifted her head. There were tears in her eyes, making them appear just as full of adjectives as any protagonist's.

Broody suddenly realized he was having a hard time swallowing.

Even.

His.

Internal narration began to stutter.

"Blondie," he said again. How different these past few days would have been without her. He'd become so proud of his book, of all that he'd achieved. But he would have never been able to do it without her. She had been more than a supporting character to him. She'd pushed him, challenged him.

Why, it was almost as if she was the Broody, and he'd been the clueless love interest all along.

Finally, he said, "You're . . . you're a main character to me."

She looked up at him. "Really?"

"Absolutely," he whispered. "You're not just an evil ex. Not to me. Not ever again."

"Hey," she said, and although she was smiling, she sounded a bit stubborn. "Hey, omniscient third person narrator? Can we get in my head for a second?"

Ah. There. Really, it was only fair if she'd spent an entire book trying to be treated like a main character that she get to have the POV, as well.

Had she done it though?

Had she really surpassed the limits of narrative, and become her own person?

She gazed at Broody, as always immune to his intense, enchanting, gemstone-colored stare, that pulled her in and . . .

Ahem. Yes. Sorry. She was TOTALLY AND COMPLETELY immune to that stare, and had no feelings for him at all, whatsoever.

Except for the way her heart did a funny little hop when he'd spoken.

Except for the way his smile made her feel.

"Oh no," she said, poking his chest. "I did not spend all book trying to get out of being in the deepest of shadows as your ex-girlfriend, just to fall for you all over again."

Broody blinked at her, confused. "You . . . fell for me? But you never . . . actually like me in our stories. Ever. You're just the evil ex. Or you were. But, Blondie, you're . . . you're a lot more than that. I realize that now."

Even if he was using sappy, silly words, they were still nice to hear. "We're all a lot more than that, Broody," she said softly, and somehow, she found herself holding his hand.

"Let's be friends," he offered shyly. "But real ones. Equal friends. Not main character and supporting character."

"I don't know," she said coyly. "I've never been friends with an Author before."

The room started to fade around them, all the trappings of plot they'd always known beginning to vanish. Everything shifted, replaced by new, unknown things. Their story had changed.

Broody really had helped someone achieve main character status.

Or, maybe, she had helped him?

Really, who can say when love is involved?

It is, after all, the most powerful force in the universe.

well, actually...

Save it for the sequel, Blondie! Time for an adventure.

Well, that's it.

That's all I've got to say. For now, at least. It's been my pleasure sharing these words with you. From the very first moment your eyes fell upon my luscious, verbose prose, I knew we would share a lovely literary journey together.

I started this book to teach you how to become a main character. You, with your oddly unique combination of hobbies and your multifaceted personality. There is no way to easily label you, reader—a fact that used to bother me.

I wanted everyone to be as much of a main character as I am. A unit, reliable and sure, and slightly flavored by outdated thinking and problematic ideals. It was all I knew. Every movie, every book, every word I've ever spoken was as a simple main character.

But you see . . . Blondie and I . . . we realized something. Together.

We were just tropes before. Acting only as we knew how to act. She, forever doomed to be an antagonist, and me, forever the perfect boyfriend.

(I mean, I'll always be the perfect boyfriend. Let's not get too wild here.)

But maybe . . . maybe *you* can be more than a trope. Don't let yourself be defined by one descriptive phrase, dear reader. Don't limit your story to a collection of hastily strung together clichés. Be yourself.

That's what being a main character is all about.

So what if you're part quirky new girl and part action hero? Who cares if your love interest is actually your best friend, and not her older brother? That's part of who you are. That's part of your three-dimensional, real-person character.

And that's why I'm proud to be not just any hero, but a young adult one. When else is it more vital, and yet more of a challenge, to truly learn who you are than when you're a teenager? When anyone can be an antagonist—your teacher, your parents, your best friend—and anyone can be a hero?

You might feel like there's a dystopian world surrounding you or that you've already met the love of your life after just a few moments of smoldering eye contact, and you may very well be right.

As a teen, your main character destiny begins anew every day. Each moment could be the next chapter one in a thrilling adventure, if you let it happen. There are so many possible stories out in the world, so many brave and brilliant and good things to come. Keep reaching for them. Keep living your story.

I saved one question for last, because it's the most important one. People so often ask, what exactly is young adult fiction? Isn't it all vampires and love triangles?

I mean, I certainly would prefer it that way. As discussed, I am very, very good at love triangles. But that wouldn't be fair for all the characters out there, and all the teens those characters represent.

Young adult is so much more than any one story or any one genre could ever hope to contain.

Young adult fiction is potential captured and frozen—a bright bolt of lightning caught on the page for everyone to read. It is both universal and incredibly personal, changeable and yet constant.

People often ask me what my favorite book is, and I simply cannot say. The book I loathe the most might be the book that led to another's main character destiny. It's possible my favorite book has yet to be written.

Perhaps you're writing it right now.

xoxo,
Blondie and *Brody*

ACKNOWLEDGMENTS

First, I have to thank my family, for encouraging me to tell my stories since I was a little kid. Mom and Dad, thank you for everything. You are my heroes. Matt, Lizzy, Wesley, and Vivian, I can't wait to share this with you. Grammy, you've been a fan of my stories since I could talk. Aunt Joan, thank you for always believing in me. To the rest of my magical, wonderful, incredible extended family, I cannot fit all of you in this book. But I am so incredibly glad you're part of my life! You have helped me become the storyteller I am. And to all the family that's in heaven . . . well, this book is for you, too.

This book would be nothing without the dedication of my agent, the talent of my editor, and the support of the whole Sky Pony team.

Linnea, I've been a fan of your work for years. We've worked together on art since before I even signed with my agent! The day you sent that first cover sketch over was the first day it really, really felt like a book.

Ellen and Delia, thank you for all the support and encouragement. That day you urged me to read my tweets out loud at dinner was the first time I truly realize how much fun it was to make people laugh with Broody.

Lindsey, thank you for believing in me ever since the Pitch Wars days. Nicole, your support is as deep as the Lake Effect snow that brought us together. Laura, this book would not exist without you, without your welcoming dinner table and late night talks over tea. Ashley, your magical copy edits are the least of your many talents. Dvorah, your friendship means so much. Patrick, thank GOODNESS we talked about writing that first time we hung out so I knew to befriend you. Leah, my internship boss turned friend, thank you. Lily, agent sister and friend, thank you.

Stephanie, Josh, and the rest of the Pittsburgh crew, you rock. To all my professors and teachers throughout the years, thank you. Ms. Soplop, thank you for reading that first manuscript in 6th grade!

Greg, thank you for befriending me at my grouchiest and introducing me to the R/YA writers group. You all are amazing. Grace, your DM about art, and our subsequent work together was a serious highlight.

Sam! You were there to share in the good news. Thank you for everything.

Holly, thank you for volunteering to be a mentor. Your emails have provided so much support and guidance to me.

Zorida, for hosting my cover reveal, and guiding me through my first author interview. To the incredible, dream authors who blurbed, I can't say thank you enough.

To the lovely authors and librarians I met at YALSA, the day after I sold my book. Thank you for welcoming me and sharing in my joy. Dahlia, thank you.

Christy, you are literal sunshine. Sil, I learn so much from you. Thank you both for being the best captains in the world.

To all BroodyBFFs, thank you! I can't tell you how much joy your posts, tweets, art, and words have brought to me. Thank you!

2017 Debuts, you are a lovely group of supportive people. Patty, thanks for putting up with the non-stop mail pre-launch! Danielle, you are a sanity saver. Melissa, thank you for your beautiful work. Aentee, your graphic design skills rock.

Megan, my childhood wouldn't have been the same without your friendship. Thank you. Ana. Alina, Kyra, I am so honored to be your Mom-Friend. Thank you for reminding me of all the magic YA has to offer its readers.

Market Street Grocery, thank you for being my absolute favorite place to write.

Thank you to everyone who I haven't been able to name. Your support matters so much, and you are truly a wonderful person (and I'll probably write you a long apology if I realize I forgot you.) Thank you to every librarian in the world, getting books and so much more to children who need them.

And a final thank you to every one of Broody's followers. Every one of you, I promise, I see you. You matter. You are always a main character.